THE LAST MYSTERY OF A LOST WORLD

Out of the night it came, a hideous-looking creature with huge wings, bulging eyes, and the face of a human. To the gallant band of men, trapped on the time-forgotten continent of Caprona and long accustomed to horrors beyond description, it was the most gruesome sight of all.

This is the tale of how the leader of the group, Bradley, was carried off by the flying men of Caprona, and deposited into the clutches of the diabolical Wieroos—who used the skulls of their victims to pave the streets of their city.

FOREWORD

Young traveler and adventurer Bowen Tyler has been marooned with his wife on *Caspak,* a mysterious and uncharted land far in the southern seas. Here Time's laws have been reversed, and the denizens of a thousand lost ages struggle for supremacy. Amidst these terrors, Bowen Tyler seeks to find and rescue his lovely wife.

By an uncanny stroke of luck, Tyler has contacted the outside world. To his aid came Tom Billings in a powerful seaplane, flying over the unscalable cliffs that wall *Caspak* from the world. But the tropic jungles of this weird valley are alive with a thousand dangers, and Billings, too, has become lost, leaving his associates, Bradley and the others, behind at the hastily-constructed "Fort Dinosaur" to await his return with Bowen Tyler.

Bradley refuses to wait any longer. He decides to set out with his crew of rugged seamen and find the lost adventurers on his own. In this savage land of primeval monsters, death awaits the unwary traveler in a thousand terrible forms, and he fears that Billings may have fallen before one of the savage reptiles, or the even more savage ape-men.

This is one of Edgar Rice Burroughs' most exciting adventure novels. It was originally published as a sequel to his *The People That Time Forgot,* but unlike most sequels it can be completely enjoyed on its own, even without one's having read the previous novel. In *Caspak,* the strange land where Time stood still, Burroughs made one of his most imaginative creations and wrote an unforgettable story of thrilling adventure.

— LIN CARTER

EDGAR RICE BURROUGHS

OUT OF
TIME'S ABYSS

ace books
A Division of Charter Communications Inc.
1120 Avenue of the Americas
New York, N.Y. 10036

This Ace edition of *Out of Time's Abyss* follows the text of the original novel first published in the December, 1918 issue of Blue Book Magazine.

First Ace printing: October, 1963
Second Ace printing: November, 1969
Third Ace printing: March, 1973

Printed in U.S.A.

CHAPTER ONE

THIS IS the tale of Bradley after he left Fort Dinosaur upon the west coast of the great lake that is in the center of the island.

Upon the fourth day of September, 1916, he set out with four companions, Sinclair, Brady, James, and Tippet, to search along the base of the barrier cliffs for a point at which they might be scaled.

Through the heavy Caspakian air, beneath the swollen sun, the five men marched northwest from Fort Dinosaur, now waist-deep in lush, jungle grasses starred with myriad gorgeous blooms, now across open meadow-land and parklike expanses and again plunging into dense forests of eucalyptus and acacia and giant arboreous ferns with feathered fronds waving gently a hundred feet above their heads.

About them upon the ground, among the trees and in the air over them moved and swung and soared the countless forms of Caspak's teeming life. Always were they menaced by some frightful thing and seldom were their rifles cool, yet even in the brief time they had dwelt upon Caprona they had become callous to danger, so that they swung along laughing and chatting like soldiers on a summer hike.

"This reminds me of South Clark Street," remarked Brady, who had once served on the traffic squad in Chicago; and as no one asked him why, he volunteered that it was "because it's no place for an Irishman."

"South Clark Street and heaven have something in common, then," suggested Sinclair. James and Tippet laughed, and then a hideous growl broke from a dense thicket ahead and diverted their attention to other matters.

"One of them behemoths of 'Oly Writ," muttered Tippet as they came to a halt and with guns ready awaited the almost inevitable charge.

"Hungry lot o' beggars, these," said Bradley; "always trying to eat everything they see."

For a moment no further sound came from the thicket. "He may be feeding now," suggested Bradley. "We'll try to go around him. Can't waste ammunition. Won't last forever. Follow me." And he set off at right angles to their former course, hoping to avert a charge. They had taken a dozen steps, perhaps, when the thicket moved to the advance of the thing within it, the leafy branches parted, and the hideous head of a gigantic bear emerged.

"Pick your trees," whispered Bradley. "Can't waste ammunition."

The men looked about them. The bear took a couple of steps forward, still growling menacingly. He was exposed to the shoulders now. Tippet took one look at the monster and bolted for the nearest tree; and then the bear charged. He charged straight for Tippet. The other men scattered for the various trees they had selected—all except Bradley. He stood watching Tippet and the bear. The man had a good start and the tree was not far away; but the speed of the enormous creature behind him was something to marvel at, yet Tippet was in a fair way to make his sanctuary when his foot caught in a tangle of roots and down he went, his rifle flying from his hand and falling several yards away. Instantly Bradley's piece was at his shoulder, there was a sharp report answered by a roar of mingled rage and pain from the carnivore. Tippet attempted to scramble to his feet.

"Lie still!" shouted Bradley. "Can't waste ammunition."

The bear halted in its tracks, wheeled toward Bradley and then back again toward Tippet. Again the former's rifle spit angrily, and the bear turned again in his direction. Bradley shouted loudly. "Come on, you behemoth of Holy Writ!" he cried. "Come on, you duffer! Can't waste ammunition." And as he saw the bear apparently upon the verge of deciding to charge him, he encouraged the idea by backing rapidly away, knowing that an angry beast will more often charge one who moves than one who lies still.

And the bear did charge. Like a bolt of lightning he flashed down upon the Englishman. "Now run!" Bradley called to Tippet and himself turned in flight toward a nearby tree. The other men, now safely ensconced upon various branches, watched the race with breathless interest. Would Bradley make it? It seemed scarce possible. And if he didn't! James gasped at the thought. Six feet at the shoulder stood the frightful mountain of blood-mad flesh and bone and sinew that was bearing down with the speed of an express train upon the seemingly slow-moving man.

It all happened in a few seconds; but they were seconds that seemed like hours to the men who watched. They saw Tippet leap to his feet at Bradley's shouted warning. They saw him run, stooping

11

to recover his rifle as he passed the spot where it had fallen. They saw him glance back toward Bradley, and then they saw him stop short of the tree that might have given him safety and turn back in the direction of the bear. Firing as he ran, Tippet raced after the great cave bear—the monstrous thing that should have been extinct ages before—ran for it and fired even as the beast was almost upon Bradley. The men in the trees scarcely breathed. It seemed to them such a futile thing for Tippet to do, and Tippet of all men! They had never looked upon Tippet as a coward—there seemed to be no cowards among that strangely assorted company that Fate had gathered together from the four corners of the earth—but Tippet was considered a cautious man. Overcautious, some thought him. How futile he and his little pop-gun appeared as he dashed after that living engine of destruction! But, oh, how glorious! It was some such thought as this that ran through Brady's mind, though articulated it might have been expressed otherwise, albeit more forcefully.

Just then it occurred to Brady to fire and he, too, opened upon the bear, but at the same instant the animal stumbled and fell forward, though still growling most fearsomely. Tippet never stopped running or firing until he stood within a foot of the brute, which lay almost touching Bradley and was already struggling to regain its feet. Placing the muzzle of his gun against the bear's ear, Tippet pulled the trigger. The creature sank limply to the ground and Bradley scrambled to his feet.

"Good work, Tippet," he said. "Mightily obliged to you—awful waste of ammunition, really."

And then they resumed the march and in fifteen

minutes the encounter had ceased even to be a topic of conversation.

For two days they continued upon their perilous way. Already the cliffs loomed high and forbidding close ahead without sign of break to encourage hope that somewhere they might be scaled. Late in the afternoon the party crossed a small stream of warm water upon the sluggishly moving surface of which floated countless millions of tiny green eggs surrounded by a light scum of the same color, though of a darker shade. Their past experience of Caspak had taught them that they might expect to come upon a stagnant pool of warm water if they followed the stream to its source; but there they were almost certain to find some of Caspak's grotesque, manlike creatures. Already since they had disembarked from the U-33 after its perilous trip through the subterranean channel beneath the barrier cliffs had brought them into the inland sea of Caspak, had they encountered what had appeared to be three distinct types of these creatures. There had been the pure apes—huge, gorillalike beasts—and those who walked a trifle more erect and had features with just a shade more of the human cast about them. Then there were men like Ahm, whom they had captured and confined at the fort—Ahm, the club-man. "Well-known club-man," Tyler had called him. Ahm and his people had knowledge of a speech. They had a language, in which they were unlike the race just inferior to them, and they walked much more erect and were less hairy: but it was principally the fact that they possessed a spoken language and carried a weapon that differentiated them from the others.

All of these peoples had proven belligerent in the

13

extreme. In common with the rest of the fauna of Caprona the first law of nature as they seemed to understand it was to kill—kill—kill. And so it was that Bradley had no desire to follow up the little stream toward the pool near which were sure to be the caves of some savage tribe; but fortune played him an unkind trick, for the pool was much closer than he imagined, its southern end reaching fully a mile south of the point at which they crossed the stream, and so it was that after forcing their way through a tangle of jungle vegetation they came out upon the edge of the pool which they had wished to avoid.

Almost simultaneously there appeared south of them a party of naked men armed with clubs and hatchets. Both parties halted as they caught sight of one another. The men from the fort saw before them a hunting party evidently returning to its caves or village laden with meat. They were large men with features closely resembling those of the African Negro though their skins were white. Short hair grew upon a large portion of their limbs and bodies, which still retained a considerable trace of apish progenitors. They were, however, a distinctly higher type than the Bo-lu, or club-men.

Bradley would have been glad to have averted a meeting; but as he desired to lead his party south around the end of the pool, and as it was hemmed in by the jungle on one side and the water on the other, there seemed no escape from an encounter.

On the chance that he might avoid a clash, Bradley stepped forward with upraised hand. "We are friends," he called in the tongue of Ahm, the Bo-lu, who had been held a prisoner at the fort; "permit us to pass in peace. We will not harm you."

At this the hatchet-men set up a great jabbering

with much laughter, loud and boisterous. "No," shouted one, "you will not harm us, for we shall kill you. Come! We kill! We kill!" And with hideous shouts they charged down upon the Europeans.

"Sinclair, you may fire," said Bradley quietly. "Pick off the leader. Can't waste ammunition."

The Englishman raised his piece to his shoulder and took quick aim at the breast of the yelling savage leaping toward them. Directly behind the leader came another hatchet-man, and with the report of Sinclair's rifle both warriors lunged forward in the tall grass, pierced by the same bullet. The effect upon the rest of the band was electrical. As one man they came to a sudden halt, wheeled to the east and dashed into the jungle, where the men could hear them forcing their way in an effort to put as much distance as possible between themselves and the authors of this new and frightful noise that killed warriors at a great distance.

Both the savages were dead when Bradley approached to examine them, and as the Europeans gathered around, other eyes were bent upon them with greater curiosity than they displayed for the victims of Sinclair's bullet. When the party again took up the march around the southern end of the pool the owner of the eyes followed them—large, round eyes, almost expressionless except for a certain cold cruelty which glinted malignly from under their pale gray irises.

All unconscious of the stalker, the men came, late in the afternoon, to a spot which seemed favorable as a campsite. A cold spring bubbled from the base of a rocky formation which overhung and partially encircled a small inclosure. At Bradley's command, the men took up the duties assigned them—gathering wood, building a cook-fire and preparing the evening meal. It was while they were thus engaged that Brady's attention was attracted by the dismal flapping of huge wings. He glanced up, expecting to see one of the great flying reptiles of a bygone age, his rifle ready in his hand. Brady was a brave man. He had groped his way up narrow tenement stairs and taken an armed maniac from a dark room without turning a hair; but now as he looked up, he went white and staggered back.

"Gawd!" he almost screamed. "What is it?"

Attracted by Brady's cry the others seized their rifles as they followed his wide-eyed, frozen gaze, nor was there one of them that was not moved by some species of terror or awe. Then Brady spoke again in an almost inaudible voice. "Holy Mother protect us—it's a banshee!"

Bradley, always cool almost to indifference in the face of danger, felt a strange, creeping sensation run over his flesh, as slowly, not a hundred feet above them, the thing flapped itself across the sky, its huge, round eyes glaring down upon them. And until it disappeared over the tops of the trees of a near-by wood the five men stood as though paralyzed, their eyes never leaving the weird shape; nor never one of them appearing to recall that he grasped a loaded rifle in his hands.

With the passing of the thing came the reaction. Tippet sank to the ground and buried his face in his hands. "Oh, Gord," he moaned. "Tyke me away from this orful plice." Brady, recovered from the first shock, swore loud and luridly. He called upon all the saints to witness that he was unafraid and that anybody with half an eye could have seen that the creature was nothing more than "one av thim flyin' alligators" that they all were familiar with.

"Yes," said Sinclair with fine sarcasm, "we've saw so many of them with white shrouds on 'em."

"Shut up, you fool!" growled Brady. "If you know so much, tell us what it was after bein' then."

Then he turned toward Bradley. "What was it, sor, do you think?" he asked.

Bradley shook his head. "I don't know," he said. "It looked like a winged human being clothed in a flowing white robe. Its face was more human than otherwise. That is the way it looked to me; but what it really was I can't even guess, for such a creature is as far beyond my experience of knowledge as it is beyond yours. All that I am sure of is that whatever else it may have been, it was quite material—it was no ghost; rather just another of the strange forms of life which we have met here and with which we should be accustomed by this time."

Tippet looked up. His face was still ashy. "Yer cawn't tell me," he cried. "Hi seen hit. Blime, Hi seen hit. Hit was ha dead man flyin' through the hair. Didn't Hi see 'is heyes? Oh, Gord! Didn't Hi see 'em?"

"It didn't look like any beast or reptile to me," spoke up Sinclair. "It was lookin' right down at me when I looked up and I saw its face plain as I see yours. It had big round eyes that looked all cold and dead, and its cheeks were sunken in deep, and I could see its yellow teeth behind thin, tight-drawn lips—like a man who had been dead a long while, sir," he added, turning toward Bradley.

"Yes!" James had not spoken since the apparition had passed over them, and now it was scarce speech which he uttered—rather a series of articulate gasps. "Yes—dead—a—long—while. It—means something. It—come—for some—one. For one—of us. One

17

—of us is goin'—to die. I'm goin' to die!" he ended in a wail.

"Come! Come!" snapped Bradley. "Won't do. Won't do at all. Get to work, all of you. Waste of time. Can't waste time."

His authoritative tones brought them all up standing, and presently each was occupied with his own duties; but each worked in silence and there was no singing and no bantering such as had marked the making of previous camps. Not until they had eaten and to each had been issued the little ration of smoking tobacco allowed after each evening meal did any sign of a relaxation of taut nerves appear. It was Brady who showed the first signs of returning good spirits. He commenced humming "It's a Long Way to Tipperary" and presently to voice the words, but he was well into his third song before anyone joined him, and even then there seemed a dismal note in even the gayest of tunes.

A huge fire blazed in the opening of their rocky shelter that the prowling carnivora might be kept at bay; and always one man stood on guard, watchfully alert against a sudden rush by some maddened beast of the jungle. Beyond the fire, yellow-green spots of flame appeared, moved restlessly about, disappeared and reappeared, accompanied by a hideous chorus of screams and growls and roars as the hungry meat-eaters hunting through the night were attracted by the light or the scent of possible prey.

But to such sights and sounds as these the five men had become callous. They sang or talked as unconcernedly as they might have done in the barroom of some publichouse at home.

Sinclair was standing guard. The others were listening to Brady's description of traffic congestion at the Rush Street bridge during the rush hour at night. The fire crackled cheerily. The owners of the yellow-green eyes raised their frightful chorus to the heavens. Conditions seemed again to have returned to normal. And then, as though the hand of Death had reached out and touched them all, the five men tensed into sudden rigidity.

Above the nocturnal diapason of the teeming jungle sounded a dismal flapping of wings and over head, through the thick night, a shadowy form passed across the diffused light of the flaring campfire. Sinclair raised his rifle and fired. An eerie wail floated down from above and the apparition, whatever it might have been, was swallowed by the darkness. For several seconds the listening men heard the sound of those dismally flapping wings lessening in the distance until they could no longer be heard.

Bradley was the first to speak. "Shouldn't have fired, Sinclair," he said; "can't waste ammunition." But there was no note of censure in his tone. It was as though he understood the nervous reaction that had compelled the other's act.

"I couldn't help it, sir," said Sinclair. "Lord, it would take an iron man to keep from shootin' at that awful thing. Do you believe in ghosts, sir?"

"No," replied Bradley. "No such things."

"I don't know about that," said Brady. "There was a woman murdered over on the prairie near Brighton—her throat was cut from ear to ear, and—"

"Shut up," snapped Bradley.

"My gran'daddy used to live down Coppington wy," said Tippet. "They were a hold ruined castle on a 'ill near by, hand at midnight they used to see pale blue lights through the windows an 'ear—"

"Will you close your hatch!" demanded Bradley. "You fools will have yourselves scared to death in a minute. Now go to sleep."

But there was little sleep in camp that night until utter exhaustion overtook the harassed men toward morning; nor was there any return of the weird creature that had set the nerves of each of them on edge.

The following forenoon the party reached the base of the barrier cliffs and for two days marched northward in an effort to discover a break in the frowning abutment that raised its rocky face almost perpendicularly above them, yet nowhere was there the slightest indication that the cliffs were scalable.

Disheartened, Bradley determined to turn back toward the fort, as he already had exceeded the time decided upon by Bowen Tyler and himself for the expedition. The cliffs for many miles had been trending in a northeasterly direction, indicating to Bradley that they were approaching the northern extremity of the island. According to the best of his calculations they had made sufficient easting during the past two days to have brought them to a point almost directly north of Fort Dinosaur and as nothing could be gained by retracing their steps along the base of the cliffs he decided to strike due south through the unexplored country between them and the fort.

That night(September 9, 1916), they made camp a short distance from the cliffs beside one of the numerous cool springs that are to be found within Caspak, oftentimes close beside the still more numerous warm and hot springs which feed the many pools. After supper the men lay smoking and chatting among themselves. Tippet was on guard. Fewer night prowlers threatened them, and the men were commenting upon the fact that the farther north they had traveled the smaller the number of all species of animal life became, though it was still present in what would have seemed appalling plenitude in any other part of the world. The diminution in reptilian life was the most noticeable change in the fauna of northern Caspak. Here, however, were forms they had not met elsewhere several of which were of gigantic proportions.

According to their custom all, with the exception of the man on guard, sought sleep early, nor, once disposed upon the ground for slumber, were they long in finding it. It seemed to Bradley that he had scarcely closed his eyes when he was brought to his feet, wide awake, by a piercing scream which was punctuated by the sharp report of a rifle from the direction of the fire where Tippet stood guard. As he ran toward the man, Bradley heard above him the same uncanny wail that had set every nerve on edge several nights before, and the dismal flapping of huge wings. He did not need to look up at the white-shrouded figure winging slowly away into the night to know that their grim visitor had returned.

The muscles of his arm, reacting to the sight and sound of the menacing form, carried his hand to the butt of his pistol; but after he had drawn the weapon, he immediately returned it to its holster with a shrug.

"What for?" he muttered. "Can't waste ammunition." Then he walked quickly to where Tippet lay sprawled upon his face. By this time James, Brady and Sinclair were at his heels, each with his rifle in readiness.

"Is he dead, sir?" whispered James as Bradley kneeled beside the prostrate form.

Bradley turned Tippet over on his back and

pressed an ear close to the other's heart. In a moment he raised his head. "Fainted," he announced. "Get water. Hurry!" Then he loosened Tippet's shirt at the throat and when the water was brought, threw a cupful in the man's face. Slowly Tippet regained consciousness and sat up. At first he looked curiously into the faces of the men about him; then an expression of terror overspread his features. He shot a startled glance up into the black void above and then burying his face in his arms began to sob like a child.

"What's wrong, man?" demanded Bradley. "Buck up! Can't play cry-baby. Waste of energy. What happened?"

"Wot 'appened, sir!" wailed Tippet. "Oh, Gord, sir! Hit came back. Hit came for me, sir. Right hit did, sir; strite hat me, sir; hand with long w'ite 'ands it clawed for me. Oh, Gord! Hit almost caught me, sir. Hi'm has good as dead; Hi'm a marked man; that's wot Hi ham. Hit was a-goin' for to carry me horf, sir."

"Stuff and nonsense," snapped Bradley. "Did you get a good look at it?"

Tippet said that he did—a much better look than he wanted. The thing had almost clutched him, and he had looked straight into its eyes—"dead heyes in a dead face," he had described them.

"Wot was it after bein', do you think?" inquired Brady.

"Hit was Death," moaned Tippet, shuddering, and again a pall of gloom fell upon the little party.

The following day Tippet walked as one in a trance. He never spoke except in reply to a direct question, which more often than not had to be repeated before it could attract his attention. He insisted that he was already a dead man, for if the thing didn't come for him during the day he would never live through another night of agonized apprehension, waiting for the frightful end that he was positive was in store for him. "I'll see to that," he said, and they all knew that Tippet meant to take his own life before darkness set in.

Bradley tried to reason with him, in his short, crisp way, but soon saw the futility of it; nor could he take the man's weapons from him without subjecting him to almost certain death from any of the numberless dangers that beset their way.

The entire party was moody and glum. There was none of the bantering that had marked their intercourse before, even in the face of blighting hardships and hideous danger. This was a new menace that threatened them, something that they couldn't explain; and so, naturally, it aroused within them superstitious fear which Tippet's attitude only tended to augment. To add further to their gloom, their way led through a dense forest, where, on account of the underbrush, it was difficult to make even a mile an hour. Constant watchfulness was required to avoid the many snakes of various degrees of repulsiveness and enormity that infested the wood; and the only ray of hope they had to cling to was that the forest would, like the majority of Caspakian forests, prove to be of no considerable extent.

Bradley was in the lead when he came suddenly upon a grotesque creature of Titanic proportions. Crouching among the trees, which here commenced to thin out slightly, Bradley saw what appeared to be an enormous dragon devouring the carcass of a mammoth. From frightful jaws to the tip of its long tail it was fully forty feet in length. Its body was covered with plates of thick skin which bore a striking resemblance to armor-plate. The creature saw

Bradley almost at the same instant that he saw it and reared up on its enormous hind legs until its head towered a full twenty-five feet above the ground. From the cavernous jaws issued a hissing sound of a volume equal to the escaping steam from the safety-valves of half a dozen locomotives, and then the creature came for the man.

"Scatter!" shouted Bradley to those behind him; and all but Tippet heeded the warning. The man stood as though dazed, and when Bradley saw the other's danger, he too stopped and wheeling about sent a bullet into the massive body forcing its way through the trees toward him. The shot struck the creature in the belly where there was no protecting armor, eliciting a new note which rose in a shrill whistle and ended in a wail. It was then that Tippet appeared to come out of his trance, for with a cry of terror he turned and fled to the left. Bradley, seeing that he had as good an opportunity as the others to escape, now turned his attention to extricating himself; and as the woods seemed dense on the right, he ran in that direction, hoping that the close-set boles would prevent pursuit on the part of the great reptile. The dragon paid no further attention to him, however, for Tippet's sudden break for liberty had attracted its attention; and after Tippet it went, bowling over small trees, uprooting underbrush and leaving a wake behind it like that of a small tornado.

Bradley, the moment he had discovered the thing was pursuing Tippet, had followed it. He was afraid to fire for fear of hitting the man, and so it was that he came upon them at the very moment that the monster lunged its great weight forward upon the doomed man. The sharp, three-toed talons of the forelimbs seized poor Tippet, and Bradley saw the unfortunate fellow lifted high above the ground as

24

the creature again reared up on its hind legs, immediately transferring Tippet's body to its gaping jaws, which closed with sickening, crunching sound as Tippet's bones cracked beneath the great teeth.

Bradley half raised his rifle to fire again and then lowered it with a shake of his head. Tippet was beyond succor—why waste a bullet that Caspak could never replace? If he could now escape the further notice of the monster it would be a wiser act than to throw his life away in futile revenge. He saw that the reptile was not looking in his direction, and so he slipped noiselessly behind the bole of a large tree and thence quietly faded away in the direction he believed the others to have taken. At what he considered a safe distance he halted and looked back. Half hidden by the intervening trees he still could see the huge head and the massive jaws from which protruded the limp legs of the dead man. Then, as though struck by the hammer of Thor, the creature collapsed and crumpled to the ground. Bradley's single bullet, penetrating the body through the soft skin of the belly, had slain the Titan.

A few minutes later, Bradley found the others of the party. The four returned cautiously to the spot where the creature lay and after convincing themselves that it was quite dead, came close to it. It was an arduous and gruesome job extricating Tippet's mangled remains from the powerful jaws, the men working for the most part silently.

"It was the work of the banshee all right," muttered Brady. "It warned poor Tippet, it did."

"Hit killed him, that's wot hit did, hand hit'll kill some more of us," said James, his lower lip trembling.

"If it was a ghost," interjected Sinclair, "and I

don't say as it was; but if it was, why, it could take on any form it wanted to. It might have turned itself into this thing, which ain't no natural thing at all, just to get poor Tippet. If it had of been a lion or something else humanlike it wouldn't look so strange; but this here thing ain't humanlike. There ain't no such thing an' never was."

"Bullets don't kill ghosts," said Bradley, "so this couldn't have been a ghost. Furthermore, there are no such things. I've been trying to place this creature. Just succeeded. It's a tyrannosaurus. Saw picture of skeleton in magazine. There's one in New York Natural History Museum. Seems to me it said it was found in place called Hell Creek somewhere in western North America. Supposed to have lived about six million years ago."

"Hell Creek's in Montana," said Sinclair. "I used to punch cows in Wyoming, an' I've heard of Hell Creek. Do you s'pose that there thing's six million years old?" His tone was skeptical.

"No," replied Bradley; "But it would indicate that the island of Caprona has stood almost without change for more than six million years."

The conversation and Bradley's assurance that the creature was not of supernatural origin helped to raise a trifle the spirits of the men; and then came another diversion in the form of ravenous meat-eaters attracted to the spot by the uncanny sense of smell which had apprised them of the presence of flesh, killed and ready for the eating.

It was a constant battle while they dug a grave and consigned all that was mortal of John Tippet to his last, lonely resting-place. Nor would they leave then; but remained to fashion a rude headstone from a crumbling out-cropping of sandstone and to gather a mass of the gorgeous flowers growing in such great profusion around them and heap the new-made grave with bright blooms. Upon the headstone Sinclair scratched in rude characters the words:

HERE LIES JOHN TIPPET
ENGLISHMAN
KILLED BY TYRANNOSAURUS
10 SEPT. A.D. 1916
R.I.P.

and Bradley repeated a short prayer before they left their comrade forever.

For three days the party marched due south through forests and meadow-land and great parklike areas where countless herbivorous animals grazed—deer and antelope and bos and the little *ecca*, the smallest species of Caspakian horse, about the size of a rabbit. There were other horses too; but all were small, the largest being not above eight hands in height. Preying continually upon the herbivora were the meat-eaters, large and small—wolves, hyaenadons, panthers, lions, tigers, and bear as well as several large and ferocious species of reptilian life.

On September twelfth the party scaled a line of sandstone cliffs which crossed their route toward the south; but they crossed them only after an encounter with the tribe that inhabited the numerous caves which pitted the face of the escarpment. That night they camped upon a rocky plateau which was sparsely wooded with jarrah, and here once again they were visited by the weird, nocturnal apparition that had already filled them with a nameless terror.

As on the night of September ninth the first warning came from the sentinel standing guard over his sleeping companions. A terror-stricken cry punctuated by the crack of a rifle brought Bradley, Sinclair and Brady to their feet in time to see James, with clubbed rifle, battling with a white-robed figure that hovered on widespread wings on a level with the Englishman's head. As they ran, shouting, forward, it was obvious to them that the weird and terrible apparition was attempting to seize James; but when it saw the others coming to his rescue, it desisted, flapping rapidly upward and away, its long, ragged wings giving forth the peculiarly dismal notes which always characterized the sound of its flying.

Bradley fired at the vanishing menacer of their peace and safety; but whether he scored a hit or not, none could tell, though, following the shot, there was wafted back to them the same piercing wail that had on other occasions frozen their marrow.

Then they turned toward James, who lay face downward upon the ground, trembling as with ague. For a time he could not even speak, but at last regained sufficient composure to tell them how the thing must have swooped silently upon him from above and behind as the first premonition of danger he had received was when the long, clawlike fingers had clutched him beneath either arm. In the mêlée his rifle had been discharged and he had broken away at the same instant and turned to defend himself with the butt. The rest they had seen.

From that instant James was an absolutely broken man. He maintained with shaking lips that his doom was sealed, that the thing had marked him for its own, and that he was as good as dead, nor could any amount of argument or raillery convince him to the contrary. He had seen Tippet marked and claimed, and now he had been marked. Nor were his constant reiterations of this belief without effect upon the rest of the party. Even Bradley felt depressed, though for the sake of the others he managed to hide it beneath a show of confidence he was far from feeling.

And on the following day William James was killed by a saber-tooth tiger—September 13, 1916. Beneath a jarrah tree on the stony plateau on the northern edge of the Sto-lu country in the land that Time forgot, he lies in a lonely grave marked by a rough headstone.

Southward from his grave marched three grim and silent men. To the best of Bradley's reckoning they were some twenty-five miles north of Fort Dinosaur, and that they might reach the fort on the following day, they plodded on until darkness overtook them. With comparative safety fifteen miles away, they made camp at last; but there was no singing now and no joking. In the bottom of his heart each prayed that they might come safely through just this night, for they knew that during the morrow they would make the final stretch, yet the nerves of each were taut with strained anticipation of what gruesome thing might flap down upon them from the black sky, marking another for its own. Who would be the next?

As was their custom, they took turns at guard, each man doing two hours and then arousing the next. Brady had gone on from eight to ten, followed by Sinclair from ten to twelve, then Bradley had been awakened. Brady would stand the last guard from two to four, as they had determined to start the moment that it became light enough to insure comparative safety upon the trail.

The snapping of a twig aroused Brady out of a dead sleep, and as he opened his eyes, he saw that it was broad daylight and that at twenty paces from him stood a huge lion. As the man sprang to his feet, his rifle ready in his hand, Sinclair awoke and took in the scene in a single swift glance. The fire was out and Bradley was nowhere in sight. For a long moment the lion and the men eyed one another. The latter had no mind to fire if the beast minded its own affairs—they were only too glad to let it go its way if it would; but the lion was of a different mind.

Suddenly the long tail snapped stiffly erect, and as though it had been attached to two trigger fingers the two rifles spoke in unison, for both men knew this signal only too well—the immediate forerunner of a deadly charge. As the brute's head had been raised, his spine had not been visible; and so they did what they had learned by long experience was best to do. Each covered a front leg, and as the tail snapped aloft, fired. With a hideous roar the mighty flesh-eater lurched forward to the ground with both front legs broken. It was an easy accomplishment in the instant before the beast charged—after, it would have been well-nigh an impossible feat. Brady stepped close in and finished him with a shot in the base of the brain lest his terrific roarings should attract his mate or others of their kind.

Then the two men turned and looked at one another. "Where is Lieutenant Bradley?" asked Sinclair. They walked to the fire. Only a few smoking embers remained. A few feet away lay Bradley's rifle. There was no evidence of a struggle. The two men circled about the camp twice and on the last lap Brady stooped and picked up an object which had lain about ten yards beyond the fire—it was Bradley's cap. Again the two looked questioningly at one another, and then, simultaneously, both pairs of eyes swung upward and searched the sky. A moment later Brady was examining the ground about the spot where Bradley's cap had lain. It was one of those little barren, sandy stretches that they had found only upon this stony plateau. Brady's own footsteps showed as plainly as black ink upon white paper; but his was the only foot that had marred the smooth, windswept surface—there was no sign that Bradley had crossed the spot *upon the surface of the ground*, and yet his cap lay well toward the center of it.

Breakfastless and with shaken nerves the two survivors plunged madly into the long day's march. Both were strong, courageous, resourceful men; but each had reached the limit of human nerve endurance and each felt that he would rather die than spend another night in the hideous open of that frightful land. Vivid in the mind of each was a picture of Bradley's end, for though neither had witnessed the tragedy, both could imagine almost precisely what had occurred. They did not discuss it—they did not even mention it—yet all day long the thing was uppermost in the mind of each and mingled with it a similar picture with himself as victim should they fail to make Fort Dinosaur before dark.

And so they plunged forward at reckless speed, their clothes, their hands, their faces torn by the retarding underbrush that reached forth to hinder them. Again and again they fell; but be it to their credit that the one always waited and helped the other and that into the mind of neither entered the thought or the temptation to desert his companion —they would reach the fort together if both survived, or neither would reach it.

They encountered the usual number of savage beasts and reptiles; but they met them with a courageous recklessness born of desperation, and by virtue of the very madness of the chances they took, they came through unscathed and with the minimum of delay.

Shortly after noon they reached the end of the plateau. Before them was a drop of two hundred feet to the valley beneath. To the left, in the distance, they could see the waters of the great inland sea that covers a considerable portion of the area of the crater island of Caprona and at a little lesser distance to the south of the cliffs they saw a thin spiral of smoke arising above the tree-tops.

The landscape was familiar—each recognized it immediately and knew that that smoky column marked the spot where Dinosaur had stood. Was the fort still there, or did the smoke arise from the smoldering embers of the building they had helped to fashion for the housing of their party? Who could say!

Thirty precious minutes that seemed as many hours to the impatient men were consumed in locating a precarious way from the summit to the base of the cliffs that bounded the plateau upon the south, and then once again they struck off upon level ground toward their goal. The closer they approached the fort the greater became their apprehension that all would not be well. They pictured the barracks deserted or the small company massacred and the buildings in ashes. It was almost in a frenzy of fear that they broke through the final fringe of jungle and stood at last upon the verge of the open meadow a half-mile from Fort Dinosaur.

"Lord!" ejaculated Sinclair. "They are still there!" And he fell to his knees, sobbing.

Brady trembled like a leaf as he crossed himself and gave silent thanks, for there before them stood the sturdy ramparts of Dinosaur and from inside the inclosure rose a thin spiral of smoke that marked the location of the cook-house. All was well, then, and their comrades were preparing the evening meal!

Across the clearing they raced as though they had not already covered in a single day a trackless, primeval country that might easily have required to days by fresh and untired men. Within hailing distance they set up such a loud shouting that presently heads appeared above the top of the parapet and soon answering shouts were rising from within Fort Dinosaur. A moment later three men issued from the inclosure and came forward to meet the survivors and listen to the hurried story of the eleven eventful days since they had set out upon their expedition to the barrier cliffs. They heard of the deaths of Tippet and James and of the disappearance of Lieutenant Bradley, and a new terror settled upon Dinosaur.

Olson, the Irish engineer, with Whitely and Wilson constituted the remnants of Dinosaur's defenders, and to Brady and Sinclair they narrated the salient events that had transpired since Bradley and his party had marched away on September 4th. They told them of the infamous act of Baron Friedrich von Schoenvorts and his German crew who had stolen the U-33, breaking their parole, and steaming away toward the subterranean opening through the barrier cliffs that carried the waters of the inland sea into the open Pacific beyond; and of the cowardly shelling of the fort.

They told of the disappearance of Miss La Rue in the night of September 11th, and of the departure of Bowen Tyler in search of her, accompanied only by his Airedale, Nobs. Thus of the original party of eleven Allies and nine Germans that had constituted the company of the U-33 when she left English waters after her capture by the crew of the English tug there were but five now to be accounted for at

Fort Dinosaur. Benson, Tippet, James, and one of the Germans were known to be dead. It was assumed that Bradley, Tyler and the girl had already succumbed to some of the savage denizens of Caspak, while the fate of the Germans was equally unknown, though it might readily be believed that they had made good their escape. They had had ample time to provision the ship and the refining of the crude oil they had discovered north of the fort could have insured them an ample supply to carry them back to Germany.

CHAPTER TWO

WHEN BRADLEY went on guard at midnight, September 14th, his thoughts were largely occupied with rejoicing that the night was almost spent without serious mishap and that the morrow would doubtless see them all safely returned to Fort Dinosaur. The hopefulness of his mood was tinged with sorrow by recollection of the two members of his party who lay back there in the savage wilderness and for whom there would never again be a homecoming.

No premonition of impending ill cast gloom over his anticipations for the coming day, for Bradley was a man who, while taking every precaution against possible danger, permitted no gloomy forebodings to weigh down his spirit. When danger threatened, he was prepared; but he was not forever courting disaster, and so it was that when about one o'clock in the morning of the fifteenth, he heard the dismal flapping of giant wings overhead, he was neither surprised nor frightened but fully prepared for an attack he had known might reasonably be expected.

The sound seemed to come from the south, and presently, low above the trees in that direction, the man made out a dim, shadowy form circling slowly about. Bradley was a brave man, yet so keen was the feeling of revulsion engendered by the sight and sound of that grim, uncanny shape that he distinctly felt the gooseflesh rise over the surface of his body and it was with difficulty that he refrained from following an instinctive urge to fire upon the nocturnal intruder. Better, far better would it have been had he given in to the insistent demand of his subconscious mentor; but his almost fanatical obsession to save ammunition proved now his undoing, for while his attention was riveted upon the thing circling before him and while his ears were filled with the beating of its wings, there swooped silently out of the black night behind him another weird and ghostly shape. With its huge wings partly closed for the dive and its white robe fluttering in its wake, the apparition swooped down upon the Englishman.

So great was the force of the impact when the thing struck Bradley between the shoulders that the man was half stunned. His rifle flew from his grasp, he felt clawlike talons of great strength seize him beneath his arms and sweep him off his feet; and then the thing rose swiftly with him, so swiftly that his cap was blown from his head by the rush of air as he was borne rapidly upward into the inky sky and the cry of warning to his companions was forced back into his lungs.

The creature wheeled immediately toward the east and was at once joined by its fellow, who circled them once and then fell in behind them. Bradley now realized the strategy that the pair had used to capture him and at once concluded that he was in the power of reasoning beings closely related to the human race if not actually of it.

Past experience suggested that the great wings were a part of some ingenious mechanical device for the limitations of the human mind, which is always loath to accept aught beyond its own little experience, would not permit him to entertain the idea that the creatures might be naturally winged and at the same time of human origin. From his position Bradley could not see the wings of his captor, nor in the darkness had he been able to examine those of the second creature closely when it circled before him. He listened for the purr of a motor or some other telltale sound that would prove the correctness of his theory. However, he was rewarded with nothing more than the constant *flap-flap*.

Presently, far below and ahead, he saw the waters of the inland sea, and a moment later he was borne over them. Then his captor did that which proved beyond doubt to Bradley that he was in the hands of human beings who had devised an almost perfect scheme of duplicating, mechanically, the wings of a bird—the thing spoke to its companion and in a language that Bradley partially understood, since he recognized words that he had learned from the savage races of Caspak. From this he judged that they were human, and being human, he knew that they could have no natural wings—for who had ever seen a human being so adorned! Therefore their wings must be mechanical. Thus Bradley reasoned—thus most of us reason; not by what might be possible; but by what has fallen within the range of our experience.

What he heard them say was to the effect that having covered half the distance the burden would now be transferred from one to the other. Bradley wondered how the exchange was to be accomplished. He knew that those giant wings would not permit the creatures to approach one another closely enough to effect the transfer in this manner; but he was soon to discover that they had other means of doing it.

He felt the thing that carried him rise to a greater altitude, and below he glimpsed momentarily the second white-robed figure; then the creature above sounded a low call, it was answered from below, and instantly Bradley felt the clutching talons release him; gasping for breath, he hurtled downward through space.

For a terrifying instant, pregnant with horror, Bradley fell; then something swooped for him from behind, another pair of talons clutched him beneath the arms, his downward rush was check within another hundred feet, and close to the surface of the sea he was again borne upward. As a hawk dives for a songbird on the wing, so this great, human bird dived for Bradley. It was a harrowing experience, but soon over, and once again the captive was being carried swiftly toward the east and what fate he could not even guess.

It was immediately following his transfer in mid-air that Bradley made out the shadowy form of a large island far ahead, and not long after, he realized that this must be the intended destination of his captors. Nor was he mistaken. Three quarters of an hour from the time of his seizure his captors dropped gently to earth in the strangest city that human eye had ever rested upon. Just a brief glimpse of his immediate surroundings vouchsafed Bradley before he was whisked into the interior of one of the buildings; but in that momentary glance he saw strange piles of stone and wood and mud fashioned into buildings of all conceivable sizes and shapes, sometimes piled high on top of one another, sometimes standing alone in an open courtway, but usually crowded and jammed together, so that there were no streets or alleys between them other than a few which ended almost as soon as they began. The principal doorways appeared to be in the roofs, and it was through one of these that Bradley was inducted into the dark interior of a low-ceiled room. Here he was pushed roughly into a corner where he tripped over a thick mat, and there his captors left him. He heard them moving about in the darkness for a moment, and several times he saw their large luminous eyes glowing in the dark. Finally, these disappeared and silence reigned, broken only by the breathing of the creatures which indicated to the Englishman that they were sleeping somewhere in the same apartment.

It was now evident that the mat upon the floor was intended for sleeping purposes and that the rough shove that had sent him to it had been a rude invitation to repose. After taking stock of himself and finding that he still had his pistol and ammunition, some matches, a little tobacco, a canteen full of water and a razor, Bradley made himself comfortable upon the mat and was soon asleep, knowing that an attempted escape in the darkness without knowledge of his surroundings would be predoomed to failure.

When he awoke, it was broad daylight, and the sight that met his eyes made him rub them again and again to assure himself that they were really open and that he was not dreaming. A broad shaft of morning light poured through the open doorway in the ceiling of the room which was about thirty feet square, or roughly square, being irregular in shape, one side curving outward, another being indented by what might have been the corner of another building jutting into it, another alcoved by three sides of an octagon, while the fourth was serpentine in contour. Two windows let in more daylight, while two doors evidently gave ingress to other rooms. The walls were partially ceiled with thin strips of wood, nicely fitted and finished, partially plastered and the rest covered with a fine, woven cloth. Figures of reptiles and beasts were painted without regard to any uniform scheme here and there upon the walls. A striking feature of the decorations consisted of several engaged columns set in the walls at no regular intervals, the captials of each supporting a human skull the cranium of which touched the ceiling, as though the latter was supported by these grim reminders either of departed relatives or of some hideous tribal rite—Bradley could not but wonder which.

Yet it was none of these things that filled him with greatest wonder—no, it was the figures of the two creatures that had captured him and brought him hither. At one end of the room a stout pole about two inches in diameter ran horizontally from wall to wall some six or seven feet from the floor, its ends securely set in two of the columns. Hanging by their knees from this perch, their heads downward and their bodies wrapped in their huge wings, slept the creatures of the night before—like two great, horrid bats they hung, asleep.

As Bradley gazed upon them in wide-eyed astonishment, he saw plainly that all his intelligence, all his acquired knowledge through years of observation and experience were set at naught by the simple evidence of the fact that stood out glaringly before his eyes—the creatures' wings were not mechanical devices but as natural appendages, growing from their shoulderblades, as were their arms and legs. He saw, too, that except for their wings the pair bore a strong resemblance to human beings, though fashioned in a most grotesque mold.

As he sat gazing at them, one of the two awoke, separated his wings to release his arms that had been folded across his breast, placed his hands upon the floor, dropped his feet and stood erect. For a moment he stretched his great wings slowly, solemnly blinking his large round eyes. Then his gaze fell upon Bradley. The thin lips drew back tightly against yellow teeth in a grimace that was nothing but hideous. It could not have been termed a smile, and what emotion it registered the Englishman was at a loss to guess. No expression whatever altered the steady gaze of those large, round eyes; there was no color upon the pasty, sunken cheeks. A death's head grimaced as though a man long dead raised his parchment-covered skull from an old grave.

The creature stood about the height of an average man but appeared much taller from the fact that the joints of his long wings rose fully a foot above his hairless head. The bare arms were long and sinewy, ending in strong, bony hands with clawlike fingers —almost talonlike in their suggestiveness. The white robe was separated in front, revealing skinny legs and the further fact that the thing wore but the single garment, which was of fine, woven cloth. From crown to sole the portions of the body exposed were entirely hairless, and as he noted this, Bradley also noted for the first time the cause of much of the seeming expressionlessness of the creature's countenance—it had neither eye-brows nor lashes. The ears were small and rested flat against the skull, which was noticeably round, though the face was quite flat. The creature had small feet, beautifully arched and plump, but so out of keeping with every other physical attribute it possessed as to appear ridiculous.

After eyeing Bradley for a moment the thing approached him. "Where from?" it asked.

"England," replied Bradley, as briefly.

"Where is England and what?" pursued the questioner.

"It is a country far from here," answered the Englishman.

"Are your people *cor-sva-jo* or *cos-ata-lu?*"

"I do not understand you," said Bradley; "and now suppose you answer a few questions. Who are you? What country is this? Why did you bring me here?"

Again the sepulchral grimace. "We are Wieroos. Luata is our father. Caspak is ours. This, our country, is called Oo-oh. We brought you here for (literally) Him Who Speaks for Luata to gaze upon and question. He would know from whence you came and why; but principally if you be *cos-ata-lu.*"

"And if I am not *cos*—whatever you call the bloomin' beast—what of it?"

The Wieroo raised his wings in a very human shrug and waved his bony claws toward the human skulls supporting the ceiling. His gesture was eloquent; but he embellished it by remarking, "And possibly if you are."

"I'm hungry," snapped Bradley.

The Wieroo motioned him to one of the doors which he threw open, permitting Bradley to pass out onto another roof on a level lower than that upon which they had landed earlier in the morning.

By daylight the city appeared even more remarkable than in the moonlight, though less weird and unreal. The houses of all shapes and sizes were piled about as a child might pile blocks of various forms and colors. He saw now that there were what might be called streets or alleys, but they ran in baffling turns and twists, nor ever reached a destination, always ending in a dead wall where some Wieroo had built a house across them.

Upon each house was a slender column supporting a human skull. Sometimes the columns were at one corner of the roof, sometimes at another, or again they rose from the center or near the center, and the columns were of varying heights, from that of a man to those which rose twenty feet above their roofs. The skulls were, as a rule, painted—blue or white, or in combinations of both colors. The most effective were painted blue with the teeth white and the eye-sockets rimmed with white.

There were other skulls—thousands of them—tens, hundreds of thousands. They rimmed the eaves of every house, they were set in the plaster of the outer walls and at no great distance from where Bradley stood rose a round tower built entirely of human skulls. And the city extended in every direction as far as the Englishman could see.

All about him Wieroos were moving across the roofs or winging through the air. The sad sound of their flapping wings rose and fell like a solemn dirge. Most of them were appareled all in white, like his captors; but others had markings of red or blue or yellow slashed across the front of their robes.

His guide pointed toward a doorway in an alley below them. "Go there and eat," he commanded, "and then come back. You cannot escape. If any question you, say that you belong to Fosh-bal-soj. There is the way." And this time he pointed to the top of a ladder which protruded above the eaves of the roof near-by. Then he turned and reentered the house.

Bradley looked about him. No, he could not escape—that seemed evident. The city appeared interminable, and beyond the city, if not a savage wilderness filled with wild beasts, there was the broad inland sea infested with horrid monsters. No wonder his captor felt safe in turning him loose in Oo-oh—he wondered if that was the name of the country or the city and if there were other cities like this upon the island.

Slowly he descended the ladder to the seemingly deserted alley which was paved with what appeared to be large, round cobblestones. He looked again at the smooth, worn pavement, and a rueful grin crossed his features—the alley was paved with skulls. "The City of Human Skulls," mused Bradley. "They must have been collectin' 'em since Adam," he thought, and then he crossed and entered the building through the doorway that had been pointed out to him.

Inside he found a large room in which were many Wieroos seated before pedestals the tops of which were hollowed out so that they resembled the ordinary bird drinking- and bathing-fonts so commonly seen on suburban lawns. A seat protruded from each of the four sides of the pedestals—just a flat board with a support running from its outer end diagonally to the base of the pedestal.

As Bradley entered, some of the Wieroos espied him, and a dismal wail arose. Whether it was a greeting or a threat, Bradley did not know. Suddenly from a dark alcove another Wieroo rushed out toward him. "Who are you?" he cried. "What do you want?"

"Fosh-bal-soj sent me here to eat," replied Bradley.

"Do you belong to Fosh-bal-soj?" asked the other.

"That appears to be what he thinks," answered the Englishman.

"Are you *cos-ata-lu?*" demanded the Wieroo.

"Give me something to eat or I'll be all of that," replied Bradley.

The Wieroo looked puzzled. "Sit here, *jaal-lu,*" he snapped, and Bradley sat down unconscious of the fact that he had been insulted by being called a hyena-man, an appellation of contempt in Caspak.

The Wieroo had seated him at a pedestal by himself, and as he sat waiting for what was next to transpire, he looked about him at the Wieroo in his immediate vicinity. He saw that in each font was a quantity of food, and that each Wieroo was armed with a wooden skewer, sharpened at one end, with which they carried solid portions of food to their mouths. At the other end of the skewer was fastened a small clam-shell. This was used to scoop up the smaller and softer portions of the repast into which all four of the occupants of each table dipped impartially. The Wieroo leaned far over their food, scooping it up rapidly and with much noise, and so great was their haste that a part of each mouthful always fell back into the common dish; and when they choked, by reason of the rapidity with which they attempted to bolt their food, they often lost it all. Bradley was glad that he had a pedestal all to himself.

Soon the keeper of the place returned with a

wooden bowl filled with food. This he dumped into Bradley's "trough," as he already thought of it. The Englishman was glad that he could not see into the dark alcove or know what were all the ingredients that constituted the mess before him, for he was very hungry.

After the first mouthful he cared even less to investigate the antecedents of the dish, for he found it peculiarly palatable. It seemed to consist of a combination of meat, fruits, vegetables, small fish and other undistinguishable articles of food all seasoned to produce a gastronomic effect that was at once baffling and delicious.

When he had finished, his trough was empty, and then he commenced to wonder who was to settle for his meal. As he waited for the proprietor to return, he fell to examining the dish from which he had eaten and the pedestal upon which it rested. The font was of stone worn smooth by long-continued use, the four outer edges hollowed and polished by the contact of the countless Wieroo bodies that had leaned against them for how long a period of time Bradley could not even guess. Everything about the place carried the impression of hoary age. The carved pedestals were black with use, the wooden seats were worn hollow, the floor of stone slabs was polished by the contact of possibly millions of naked feet and worn away in the aisles between the pedestals so that the latter rested upon little mounds of stone several inches above the general level of the floor.

Finally, seeing that no one came to collect, Bradley arose and started for the doorway. He had covered half the distance when he heard the voice of mine host calling to him. "Come back, *jaal-lu*," screamed the Wieroo; and Bradley did as he was bid. As he approached the creature which stood now behind a large, flat-topped pedestal beside the alcove, he saw lying upon the smooth surface something that almost elicited a gasp of astonishment from him—a simple, common thing it was, or would have been almost anywhere in the world but Caspak —a square bit of paper!

And on it, in a fine hand, written compactly, were many strange hieroglyphics! These remarkable creatures, then, had a written as well as a spoken language and besides the art of weaving cloth possessed that of paper-making. Could it be that such grotesque beings represented the high culture of the human race within the boundaries of Caspak? Had natural selection produced during the countless ages of Caspakian life a winged monstrosity that represented the earthly pinnacle of man's evolution?

Bradley had noted something of the obvious indications of a gradual evolution from ape to spear-man as exemplified by the several overlapping races of Alalus, club-men and hatchet-men that formed the connecting links between the two extremes with which he had come in contact. He had heard of the Krolus and the Galus—reputed to be still higher in the plane of evolution—and now he had indisputable evidence of a race possessing refinements of civilization eons in advance of the spear-men. The conjectures awakened by even a momentary consideration of the possibilities involved became at once as wildly bizarre as the insane imagings of a drug addict.

As these thoughts flashed through his mind, the Wieroo held out a pen of bone fixed to a wooden holder and at the same time made a sign that Bradley was to write upon the paper. It was difficult to judge from the expressionless features of the Wieroo what was passing in the creature's mind, but Bradley could not but feel that the thing cast a supercilious glance upon him as much as to say, "Of course you do not know how to write, you poor, low creature; but you can make your mark."

Bradley seized the pen and in a clear, bold hand wrote: "John Bradley, England." The Wieroo showed evidences of consternation as it seized the piece of paper and examined the writing with every mark of incredulity and surprise. Of course it could make nothing of the strange characters; but it evidently accepted them as proof that Bradley possessed knowledge of a written language of his own, for following the Englishman's entry it made a few characters of its own.

"You will come here again just before Lua hides his face behind the great cliff" announced the creature, "unless before that you are summoned by Him Who Speaks for Luata, in which case you will not have to eat any more."

"Reassuring cuss," thought Bradley as he turned and left the building.

Outside were several of the Wieroos that had been eating at the pedestals within. They immediately surrounded him, asking all sorts of questions, plucking at his garments, his ammunition-belt and his pistol. Their demeanor was entirely different from what it had been within the eating-place and Bradley was to learn that a house of food was sanctuary for him, since the stern laws of the Wieroos forbade altercations within such walls. Now they were rough and threatening, as with wings half spread they hovered about him in menacing attitudes, barring his way to the ladder leading to the roof from whence he had descended; but the Englishman was not one to brook interference for long. He attempted at first to push his way past them, and then when one seized his arm and jerked him roughly back, Bradley swung upon the creature and with a heavy blow to the jaw felled it.

Instantly pandemonium reigned. Loud wails arose, great wings opened and closed with a loud, beating noise and many clawlike hands reached forth to clutch him. Bradley struck to right and left. He dared not use his pistol for fear that once they discovered its power he would be overcome by weight of numbers and relieved of possession of what he considered his trump card, to be reserved until the last moment that it might be used to aid in his escape, for already the Englishman was planning, though almost hopelessly, such an attempt.

A few blows convinced Bradley that the Wieroos were arrant cowards and that they bore no weapons, for after two or three had fallen beneath his fists the others formed a circle about him, but at a safe distance, and contented themselves with threatening and blustering, while those whom he had felled lay upon the pavement without trying to arise, the while they moaned and wailed in lugubrious chorus.

Again Bradley strode toward the ladder, and this time the circle parted before him; but no sooner had he ascended a few rungs than he was seized by one foot and an effort made to drag him down. With a quick backward glance the Englishman, clinging firmly to the ladder with both hands, drew up his free foot and with all the strength of a powerful leg planted a heavy shoe squarely in the flat face of the Wieroo that held him. Shrieking horribly, the creature clapped both hands to its face and sank to the ground while Bradley clambered quickly the remaining distance to the roof, though no sooner did he reach the top of the ladder than a great flapping of wings beneath him warned him that the Wieroos were rising after him. A moment later they swarmed about his head as he ran for the apartment in which he had spent the early hours of the morning after his arrival.

It was but a short distance from the top of the ladder to the doorway, and Bradley had almost reached his goal when the door flew open and Fosh-bal-soj stepped out. Immediately the pursuing Wieroos demanded punishment of the *jaal-lu* who had so grievously maltreated them. Fosh-bal-soj listened to their complaints and then with a sudden sweep of his right hand seized Bradley by the scruff of the neck and hurled him sprawling through the doorway upon the floor of the chamber.

So sudden was the assault and so surprising the strength of the Wieroo that the Englishman was taken completely off his guard. When he arose, the door was closed, and Fosh-bal-soj was standing over him, his hideous face contorted into an expression of rage and hatred.

"Hyena, snake, lizard!" he screamed. "You would dare lay your low, vile, profaning hands upon even the lowliest of the Wieroos—the sacred, chosen of Luata!"

Bradley was mad, and so he spoke in a very low, calm voice while a half-smile played across his lips; but his cold, gray eyes were unsmiling.

"What you did to me just now," he said, "—I am going to kill you for that," and even as he spoke, he launched himself at the throat of Fosh-bal-soj. The other Wieroo that had been asleep when Bradley left the chamber had departed, and the two were alone. Fosh-bal-soj displayed little of the cowardice of those that had attacked Bradley in the alleyway, but that may have been because he had so slight opportunity, for Bradley had him by the throat before he could utter a cry and with his right hand struck him heavily and repeatedly upon his face and over his heart—ugly, smashing, short-arm jabs of the sort that take the fight out of a man in quick time.

But Fosh-bal-soj was of no mind to die passively. He clawed and struck at Bradley while with his great wings he attempted to shield himself from the merciless rain of blows, at the same time searching for a hold upon his antagonist's throat. Presently he succeeded in tripping the Englishman, and together the two fell heavily to the floor, Bradley underneath, and at the same instant the Wieroo fastened his long talons about the other's windpipe.

Fosh-bal-soj was possessed of enormous strength and he was fighting for his life. The Englishman soon realized that the battle was going against him. Already his lungs were pounding painfully for air as he reached for his pistol. It was with difficulty that he drew it from its holster, and even then, with death staring him in the face, he thought of his precious ammunition. "Can't waste it," he thought; and slipping his fingers to the barrel he raised the weapon and struck Fosh-bal-soj a terrific blow between the eyes. Instantly the clawlike fingers released their hold, and the creature sank limply to the floor beside Bradley, who lay for several minutes gasping painfully in an effort to regain his breath.

When he was able, he rose and leaned close over the Wieroo, lying silent and motionless, his wings dropping limply and his great, round eyes staring blankly toward the ceiling. A brief examination convinced Bradley that the thing was dead, and with the conviction came an overwhelming sense of the dangers which must now confront him; but how was he to escape?

His first thought was to find some means for concealing the evidence of his deed and then to make a bold effort to escape. Stepping to the second door he pushed it gently open and peered in upon what seemed to be a store room. In it was a litter of cloth such as the Wieroos' robes were fashioned from, a number of chests painted blue and white, with white hieroglyphics painted in bold strokes upon the blue and blue hieroglyphics upon the white. In one corner was a pile of human skulls reaching almost to the ceiling and in another a stack of dried Wieroo wings. The chamber was as irregularly shaped as the other and had but a single window and a second door at the further end, but was without the exit through the roof and, most important of all, there was no creature of any sort in it.

As quickly as possible Bradley dragged the dead Wieroo through the doorway and closed the door, then he looked about for a place to conceal the corpse. One of the chests was large enough to hold the body if the knees were bent well up, and with this idea in view Bradley approached the chest to open it. The lid was made in two pieces, each being hinged at an opposite end of the chest and joining nicely where they met in the center of the chest making a snug, well-fitting joint. There was no lock. Bradley raised one half the cover and looked in. With a smothered "By Jove!" he bent closer to examine the contents—the chest was about half filled with an assortment of golden trinkets. There were what appeared to be bracelets, anklets and brooches of virgin gold.

Realizing that there was no room in the chest for the body of the Wieroo, Bradley turned to seek another means of concealing the evidence of his crime. There was a space between the chests and the wall, and into this he forced the corpse, piling the discarded robes upon it until it was entirely hidden from sight; but now how was he to make good his escape in the bright glare of that early Spring day?

He walked to the door at the far end of the apartment and cautiously opened it an inch. Before him and about two feet away was the blank wall of another building. Bradley opened the door a little farther and looked in both directions. There was no one in sight to the left over a considerable expanse of roof-top, and to the right another building shut off his line of vision at about twenty feet. Slipping out, he turned to the right and in a few steps found a narrow passageway between two buildings. Turning into this he passed about half its length when he saw a Wieroo appear at the opposite end and halt. The creature was not looking down the passageway; but at any moment it might turn its eyes toward him, when he would be immediately discovered.

To Bradley's left was a triangular niche in the wall of one of the houses, and into this he dodged, thus concealing himself from the sight of the Wieroo. Beside him was a door painted a vivid yellow and constructed after the same fashion as the other Wieroo doors he had seen, being made up of countless narrow strips of wood from four to six inches in length laid on in patches of about the same width, the strips in adjacent patches never running in the same direction. The result bore some resemblance to a crazy patchwork quilt, which was heightened when, as in one of the doors he had seen, contiguous patches were painted different colors. The strips appeared to have been bound together and to the underlying framework of the door with gut or fiber and also glued, after which a thick coating of paint had been applied. One edge of the door was formed of a straight, round pole about two inches in diameter that protruded at top and bottom, the projections setting in round holes in both lintel and sill and forming the axis upon which the door swung. An eccentric disk upon the inside face of the door engaged a slot in the frame when it was desired to secure the door against intruders.

As Bradley stood flattened against the wall waiting for the Wieroo to move on, he heard the creature's wings brushing against the sides of the buildings as it made its way down the narrow passage in his direction. As the yellow door offered the only means of escape without detection, the Englishman decided to risk whatever might lie beyond it, and so, boldly pushing it in, he crossed the threshold and entered a small apartment.

As he did so, he heard a muffled ejaculation of surprise, and turning his eyes in the direction from whence the sound had come, he beheld a wide-eyed girl standing flattened against the opposite wall, an expression of incredulity upon her face. At a glance he saw that she was of no race of humans that he had come in contact with since his arrival upon Caprona—there was no trace about her form or features of any relationship to those low orders of men, nor was she appareled as they—or, rather, she did not entirely lack apparel as did most of them.

A soft hide fell from her left shoulder to just below her left hip on one side and almost to her right knee on the other, a loose girdle was about her waist, and golden ornaments such as he had seen in the blue-and-white chest encircled her arms and legs, while a golden fillet with a triangular diadem bound her heavy hair above her brows. Her skin was white as from long confinement within doors; but it was clear and fine. Her figure, but partially concealed by the soft deerskin, was all curves of symmetry and youthful grace, while her features might easily have been the envy of the most feted of Continental beauties.

If the girl was surprised by the sudden appearance of Bradley, the latter was absolutely astounded to discover so wondrous a creature among the hideous inhabitants of the City of Human Skulls. For a moment the two looked at one another in unconcealed consternation, and then Bradley spoke, using, to the best of his poor ability, the common tongue of Caspak.

"Who are you," he asked, "and from where do you come? Do not tell me that you are a Wieroo."

"No," she replied, "I am no Wieroo." And she shuddered slightly as she pronounced the word. "I am a Galu; but who and what are you? I am sure that you are no Galu, from your garments; but you are like the Galus in other respects. I know that you are not of this frightful city, for I have been here for almost ten moons, and never have I seen a male Galu brought hither before, nor are there such as you and I, other than prisoners in the land of Oo-oh, and these are all females. Are you a prisoner, then?"

He told her briefly who and what he was, though he doubted if she understood, and from her he learned that she had been a prisoner there for many months; but for what purpose he did not then learn, as in the midst of their conversation the yellow door swung open and a Wieroo with a robe slashed with yellow entered.

At sight of Bradley the creature became furious. "Whence came this reptile?" it demanded of the girl. "How long has it been here with you?"

"It came through the doorway just ahead of you," Bradley answered for the girl.

The Wieroo looked relieved. "It is well for the girl that this is so," it said, "for now only you will have to die." And stepping to the door the creature raised its voice in one of those uncanny, depressing wails.

The Englishman looked toward the girl. "Shall I kill it?" he asked, half drawing his pistol. "What is best to do?—I do not wish to endanger you."

The Wieroo backed toward the door. "Defiler!" it screamed. "You dare to threaten one of the sacred chosen of Luata!"

"Do not kill him," cried the girl, "for then there could be no hope for you. That you are here, alive, shows that they may not intend to kill you at all, and so there is a chance for you if you do not anger them; but touch him in violence and your bleached skull will top the loftiest pedestal of Oo-oh."

"And what of you?" asked Bradley.

"I am already doomed," replied the girl; "I am *cos-ata-lo*."

Cos-ata-lo! cos-ata-lu!" What did these phrases mean that they were so oft repeated by the denizens of Oo-oh? *Lu* and *lo*, Bradley knew to mean man and *woman; ata;* was employed variously to indicate life, eggs, young, reproduction and kindred subject; *cos* was a negative; but in combination they were meaningless to the European.

"Do you mean they will kill you?" asked Bradley.

"I but wish that they would," replied the girl. "My fate is to be worse than death—in just a few nights more, with the coming of the new moon."

"Poor she-snake!" snapped the Wieroo. "You are to become sacred above all other shes. He Who Speaks for Luata has chosen you for himself. Today you go to his temple"—the Wieroo used a phrase meaning literally High Place—"where you will receive the sacred commands."

The girl shuddered and cast a sorrowful glance toward Bradley. "Ah," she sighed, "if I could but see my beloved country once again!"

The man stepped suddenly close to her side before the Wieroo could interpose and in a low voice asked her if there was no way by which he might encompass her escape. She shook her head sorrowfully. "Even if we escaped the city," she replied, "there is the big water between the island of Oo-oh and the Galu shore."

"And what is beyond the city, if we could leave it?" pursued Bradley.

"I may only guess from what I have heard since I was brought here," she answered; "but by reports and chance remarks I take it to be a beautiful land in which there are but few wild beasts and no men, for only the Wieroos live upon this island and they dwell always in cities of which there are three, this being the largest. The others are at the far end of the island, which is about three marches from end to end and at its widest point about one march."

From his own experience and from what the natives on the mainland had told him, Bradley knew that ten miles was a good day's march in Caspak, owing to the fact that at most points it was a trackless wilderness and at all times travelers were beset by hideous beasts and reptiles that greatly impeded rapid progress.

The two had spoken rapidly but were now interrupted by the advent through the opening in the roof of several Wieroos who had come in answer to the alarm it of the yellow slashing had uttered.

"This *jaal-lu*," cried the offended one, "has threatened me. Take its hatchet from it and make it fast where it can do no harm until He Who Speaks for Luata has said what shall be done with it. It is one of those strange creatures that Fosh-bal-soj discovered first above the Band-lu country and followed back toward the beginning. He Who Speaks for Luata sent Fosh-bal-soj to fetch him one of the creatures, and here it is. It is hoped that it may be from another world and hold the secret of the *cos-ata-lus*."

The Wieroos approached boldly to take Bradley's "hatchet" from him, their leader having indicated the pistol hanging in its holster at the Englishman's hip, but the first one went reeling backward against his fellows from the blow to the chin which Bradley followed up with a rush and the intention to clean up the room in record time; but he had reckoned without the opening in the roof. Two were down and a great wailing and moaning was arising when reinforcements appeared from above. Bradley did not see them; but the girl did, and though she cried out a warning, it came too late for him to avoid a large Wieroo who dived headforemost for him, striking him between the shoulders and bearing him to the floor. Instantly a dozen more were piling on top of him. His pistol was wrenched from its holster and he was securely pinioned down by the weight of numbers.

At a word from the Wieroo of the yellow slashing, who evidently was a person of authority, one left and presently returned with fiber ropes with which Bradley was tightly bound.

"Now bear him to the Blue Place of Seven Skulls," directed the chief Wieroo, "and one take the word of all that has passed to Him Who Speaks for Luata."

Each of the creatures raised a hand, the back against its face, as though in salute. One seized Bradley and carried him through the yellow doorway to the roof from whence it rose upon its widespread wings and flapped off across the roof-tops and of Oo-oh with its heavy burden clutched in its long talons.

Below him Bradley could see the city stretching away to a distance on every hand. It was not as large as he had imagined, though he judged that it was at least three miles square. The houses were piled in indescribable heaps, sometimes to a height of a hundred feet. The streets and alleys were short and crooked and there were many areas where buildings had been wedged in so closely that no light could possibly reach the lowest tiers, the entire surface of the ground being packed solidly with them.

The colors were varied and startling, the architecture amazing. Many roofs were cup or saucer-shaped with a small hole in the center of each, as though they had been constructed to catch rain-water and conduct it to a reservoir beneath; but nearly all the others had the large opening in the top that Bradley had seen used by these flying men in lieu of doorways. At all levels were the myriad poles surmounted by grinning skulls; but the two most prominent features of the city were the round tower of human skulls that Bradley had noted earlier in the day and another and much larger edifice near the center of the city. As they approached it, Bradley saw that it was a huge building rising a hundred feet in height from the ground and that it stood alone in the center of what might have been called a plaza in some other part of the world. Its various parts, however, were set together with the same strange irregularity that marked the architecture of the city as a whole; and it was capped by an enormous saucer-shaped roof which projected far beyond the eaves, having the appearance of a colossal Chinese coolie hat, inverted.

The Wieroo bearing Bradley passed over one corner of the open space about the large building, revealing to the Englishman grass and trees and running water beneath. They passed the building and about five hundred yards beyond the creature alighted on the roof of a square, blue building surmounted by seven poles bearing seven skulls. This then, thought Bradley, is the Blue Place of Seven Skulls.

Over the opening in the roof was a grated covering, and this the Wieroo removed. The thing then tied a piece of fiber rope to one of Bradley's ankles and rolled him over the edge of the opening. All was dark below and for an instant the Englishman came as near to experiencing real terror as he had ever come in his life before. As he rolled off into the black abyss he felt the rope tighten about his ankle and an instant later he was stopped with a sudden jerk to swing pendulumlike, head downward. Then the creature lowered away until Bradley's head came in sudden and painful contact with the floor below, after which the Wieroo let loose of the rope entirely and the Englishman's body crashed to the wooden planking. He felt the free end of the rope dropped upon him and heard the grating being slid into place above him.

CHAPTER THREE

HALF-STUNNED Bradley lay for a minute as he had fallen and then slowly and painfully wriggled into a less uncomfortable position. He could see nothing of his surroundings in the gloom about him until after a few minutes his eyes became accustomed to the dark interior when he rolled them from side to side in survey of his prison.

He discovered himself to be in a bare room which was windowless, nor could he see any other opening than that through which he had been lowered. In one corner was a huddled mass that might have been almost anything from a bundle of rags to a dead body.

Almost immediately he had taken his bearings Bradley commenced working with his bonds. He was a man of powerful physique, and as from the first he had been imbued with a belief that the fiber ropes were too weak to hold him, he worked on with a firm conviction that sooner or later they would part to his strainings. After a matter of five minutes he was positive that the strands about his wrists were beginning to give; but he was compelled to rest then from exhaustion.

As he lay, his eyes rested upon the bundle in the corner, and presently he could have sworn that the thing moved. With eyes straining through the gloom the man lay watching the grim and sinister thing in the corner. Perhaps his overwrought nerves were playing a sorry joke upon him. He thought of this and also that his condition of utter helplessness might still further have stimulated his imagination. He closed his eyes and sought to relax his muscles and his nerves; but when he looked again, he knew that he had not been mistaken—the thing had moved; now it lay in a slightly altered form and farther from the wall. It was nearer him.

With renewed strength Bradley strained at his bonds, his fascinated gaze still glued upon the shapeless bundle. No longer was there any doubt that it moved—he saw it rise in the center several inches and then creep closer to him. It sank and arose again—a headless, hideous, monstrous thing of menace. Its very silence rendered it the more terrible.

Bradley was a brave man; ordinarily his nerves were of steel; but to be at the mercy of some unknown and nameless horror, to be unable to defend himself—it was these things that almost unstrung him, for at best he was only human. To stand in the open, even with the odds all against him; to be able to use his fists, to put up some sort of defense, to inflict punishment upon his adversary—then he could face death with a smile. It was not death that he feared now—it was that horror of the unknown that is part of the fiber of every son of woman.

Closer and closer came the shapeless mass. Bradley lay motionless and listened. What was that he heard! Breathing? He could not be mistaken—and then from out of the bundle of rags issued a hollow groan. Bradley felt his hair rise upon his head. He struggled with the slowly parting strands that held him. The thing beside him rose up higher than be-

68

ore and the Englishman could have sworn that he saw a single eye peering at him from among the tumbled cloth. For a moment the bundle remained motionless—only the sound of breathing issued from it, then there broke from it a maniacal laugh.

Cold sweat stood upon Bradley's brow as he tugged for liberation. He saw the rags rise higher and higher above him until at last they tumbled upon the floor from the body of a naked man—a thin, a bony, a hideous caricature of man, that mouthed and mummed and, wabbling upon its weak and shaking legs, crumpled to the floor again, still laughing—laughing horribly.

It crawled toward Bradley. "Food! Food!" it screamed. "There is a way out! There is a way out!"

Dragging itself to his side the creature slumped upon the Englishman's breast. "Food!" it shrilled as with its bony fingers and its teeth, it sought the man's bare throat.

"Food! There is a way out!" Bradley felt teeth upon his jugular. He turned and twisted, shaking himself free for an instant; but once more with hideous persistence the thing fastened itself upon him. The weak jaws were unable to send the dull teeth through the victim's flesh; but Bradley felt it gnawing, gnawing, gnawing, like a monstrous rat, seeking his life's blood.

The skinny arms now embraced his neck, holding the teeth to his throat against all his efforts to dislodge the thing. Weak as it was it had strength enough for this in its mad efforts to eat. Mumbling as it worked, it repeated again and again, "Food! Food! There is a way out!" until Bradley thought those two expressions alone would drive him mad.

And all but mad he was as with a final effort backed by almost maniacal strength he tore his wrists from the confining bonds and grasping the repulsive thing upon his breast hurled it halfway across the room. Panting like a spend hound Bradley worked at the thongs about his ankles while the maniac lay quivering and mumbling where it had fallen. Presently the Englishman leaped to his feet— freer than he had ever before felt in all his life though he was still hopelessly a prisoner in the Blue Place of Seven Skulls.

With his back against the wall for support, so weak the reaction left him, Bradley stood watching the creature upon the floor. He saw it move and slowly raise itself to its hands and knees, where it swayed to and fro as its eyes roved about in search of him; and when at last they found him, there broke from the drawn lips the mumbled words: "Food! Food! There is a way out!" The pitiful supplication in the tones touched the Englishman's heart. He knew that this could be no Wieroo, but possibly once a man like himself who had been cast into this pit of solitary confinement with this hideous result that might in time be his fate, also.

And then, too, there was the suggestion of hope held out by the constant reiteration of the phrase "There is a way out." Was there a way out? What did this poor thing know?

"Who are you and how long have you been here?" Bradley suddenly demanded.

For a moment the man upon the floor made no response, then mumblingly came the words: "Food! Food!"

"Stop!" commanded the Englishman—the injunction might have been barked from the muzzle of a pistol. It brought the man to a sitting posture, his hands off the ground. He stopped swaying to and fro and appeared to be startled into an attempt to master his faculties of concentration and thought.

Bradley repeated his questions sharply.

"I am An-Tak, the Galu," replied the man. "Luata alone knows how long I have been here—maybe ten moons, maybe ten moons three times"—it was the Caspakian equivalent of thirty. "I was young and strong when they brought me here. Now I am old and very weak. I am *cos-ata-lu*—that is why they have not killed me. If I tell them the secret of becoming *cos-ata-lu* they will take me out; but how can I tell them that which Luata alone knows?"

"What is *cos-ata-lu?*" demanded Bradley.

"Food! Food! There is a way out!" mumbled the Galu.

Bradley strode across the floor, seized the man by his shoulders and shook him.

"Tell me," he cried, "what is *cos-ata-lu?*"

"Food!" whimpered An-Tak.

Bradley bethought himself. His haversack had not been taken from him. In it besides his razor and knife were odds and ends of equipment and a small quantity of dried meat. He tossed a small strip of the latter to the starving Galu. An-Tak seized upon it and devoured it ravenously. It instilled new life in the man.

"What is *cos-ata-lu?*" insisted Bradley again.

An-Tak tried to explain. His narrative was often broken by lapses of concentration during which he reverted to his plaintive mumbling for food and recurrence to the statement that there was a way out; but by firmness and patience the Englishman drew out piece-meal a more or less lucid exposition of the remarkable scheme of evolution that rules in Caspak. In it he found explanations of the hitherto inexplicable. He discovered why he had seen no babes or children among the Caspakian tribes with which he had come in contact; why each more northerly tribe evinced a higher state of development than those south of them; why each tribe included individuals ranging in physical and mental characteristics from the highest of the next lower race to the lowest of the next higher, and why the women of each tribe immersed themselves morning for an hour or more in the warm pools near which the habitations of their people always were located; and, too, he discovered why those pools were almost immune from the attacks of carnivorous animals and reptiles.

He learned that all but those who were *cos-ata-lu* came up *cor-sva-jo,* or *from the beginning.* The egg from which they first developed into tadpole form was deposited, with millions of others, in one of the warm pools and with it a poisonous serum that the carnivora instinctively shunned. Down the warm stream from the pool floated the countless billions of eggs and tadpoles, developing as they drifted slowly toward the sea. Some became tadpoles in the pool, some in the sluggish stream and some not until they reached the great inland sea. In the next stage they became fishes or reptiles, An-Tak was not positive which, and in this form, always developing, they swam far to the south, where, amid the rank and teeming jungles, some of them evolved into amphibians. Always there were those whose development stopped at the fish stage, others whose development ceased when they became reptiles, while by far the greater proportion formed the food supply of the ravenous creatures of the deep.

Few indeed were those that eventually developed into baboons and then apes, which was considered by Caspakians the real beginning of evolution. From the egg, then, the individual developed slowly into a higher form, just as the frog's egg develops through various stages from a fish with gills to a frog with lungs. With that thought in mind Bradley discovered that it was not difficult to believe in the possibility of such a scheme—there was nothing new in it.

From the ape the individual, if it survived, slowly developed into the lowest order of man—the Alu—and then by degrees to Bo-lu, Sto-lu, Band-lu, Kro-lu and finally to Galu. And in each stage countless millions of other eggs were deposited in the warm pools of the various races and floated down to the great sea to go through a similar process of evolution outside the womb as develops our own young within; but in Caspak the scheme is much more inclusive, for it combines not only individual development but the evolution of species and genera. If an egg survives it goes through all the stages of development that man has passed through during the unthinkable eons since life first moved upon the earth's face.

The final stage—that which the Galus have almost attained and for which all hope—is *cos-ata-lu,* which, literally, means no-egg-man, or one who is born directly as are the young of the outer world of mammals. Some of the Galus produce *cos-ata-lu* and *cos-ata-lo* both; the Weiroos only *cos-ata-lu*—in other words all Wieroos are born male, and so they prey upon the Galus for their women and sometimes capture and torture the Galu men who are *cos-ata-lu* in an endeavor to learn the secret which they believe will give them unlimited power over all other denizens of Caspak.

No Wieroos come up from the beginning—all are

born of Wieroo fathers and Galu mothers who are *cos-ata-lo,* and there are very few of the latter owing to the long and precarious stages of development. Seven generations of the same ancestor must come up from he beginning before a *cos-ata-lu* child may be born; and when one considers the frightful dangers that surround the vital spark from the moment it leaves the warm pool where it has been deposited to float down to the sea amid the voracious creatures that swarm the surface and the deeps and the almost equally unthinkable trials of its efforts to survive after it once becomes a land animal and starts northward through the horrors of the Caspakian jungles and forests, it is plainly a wonder that even a single babe has ever been born to a Galu woman.

Seven cycles it requires before the seventh Galu can complete the seventh danger-infested circle since its first Galu ancestor achieved the state of Galu. For ages before, the ancestors of this first Galu may have developed from a Band-lu or Bo-lu egg without ever once completing the whole circle—that is from a Galu egg, back to a fully developed Galu.

Bradley's head was whirling before he even commenced to grasp the complexities of Caspakian evolution; but as the truth slowly filtered into his understanding—as gradually it became possible for him to visualize the scheme, it appeared simpler. In fact, it seemed even less difficult of comprehension than that with which he was familiar.

For several minutes after An-Tak ceased speaking, his voice having trailed off weakly into silence, neither spoke again. Then the Galu recommenced his, "Food! Food! There is a way out!" Bradley tossed him another bit of dried meat, waiting patiently until he had eaten it, this time more slowly.

"What do you mean by saying there is a way out?" he asked.

"He who died here just after I came, told me," replied An-Tak. "He said there was a way out, that he had discovered it but was too weak to use his knowledge. He was trying to tell me how to find it when he died. Oh, Luata, if he had lived but a moment more!"

"They do not feed you here?" asked Bradley.

"No, they give me water once a day—that is all."

"But how have you lived, then?"

"The lizards and the rats," replied An-Tak. "The lizards are not so bad; but the rats are foul to taste. However, I must eat them or they would eat me, and they are better than nothing; but of late they do not come so often, and I have not had a lizard for a long time. I shall eat though," he mumbled. "I shall eat now, for you cannot remain awake forever." He laughed, a cackling, dry laugh. "When you sleep, An-Tak will eat."

It was horrible. Bradley shuddered. For a long time each sat in silence. The Englishman could guess why the other made no sound—he awaited the moment that sleep should overcome his victim. In the long silence there was born upon Bradley's ears a faint, monotonous sound as of running water. He listened intently. It seemed to come from far beneath the floor.

"What is that noise?" he asked. "That sounds like water running through a narrow channel."

"It is the river," replied An-Tak. "Why do you not go to sleep? It passes directly beneath the Blue Place of Seven Skulls. It runs through the temple grounds, beneath the temple and under the city. When we die, they will cut off our heads and throw our bodies into the river. At the mouth of the river await many large reptiles. Thus do they feed. The Wieroos do likewise with their own dead, keeping only the skulls and the wings. Come, let us sleep."

"Do the reptiles come up the river into the city?" asked Bradley.

"The water is too cold—they never leave the warm water of the great pool," replied An-Tak.

"Let us search for the way out," suggested Bradley.

An-Tak shook his head. "I have searched for it all these moons," he said. "If I could not find it, how would you?"

Bradley made no reply but commenced a diligent examination of the walls and floor of the room, pressing over each square foot and tapping with his knuckles. About six feet from the floor he discovered a sleeping-perch near one end of the apartment. He asked An-Tak about it, but the Galu said that no Wieroo had occupied the place since he had been incarcerated there. Again and again Bradley went over the floor and walls as high up as he could reach. Finally he swung himself to the perch, that he might examine at least one end of the room all the way to the ceiling.

In the center of the wall close to the top, an area about three feet square gave forth a hollow sound when he rapped upon it. Bradley felt over every square inch of that area with the tips of his fingers. Near the top he found a small round hole a trifle larger in diameter than his forefinger, which he immediately stuck into it. The panel, if such it was, seemed about an inch thick, and beyond it his finger encountered nothing. Bradley crooked his finger upon the opposite side of the panel and pulled toward him, steadily but with considerable force. Suddenly the panel flew inward, nearly precipitating he man to the floor. It was hinged at the bottom, and when lowered the outer edge rested upon the perch, making a little platform parallel with the floor of the room.

Beyond the opening was an utterly dark void. The Englishman leaned through it and reached his arm as far as possible into the blackness but touched nothing. Then he fumbled in his haversack for a match, a few of which remained to him. When he struck it, An-Tak gave a cry of terror. Bradley held the light far into the opening before him and in its flickering rays saw the top of a ladder descending into a black abyss below. How far down it extended he could not guess; but that he should soon know definitely he was positive.

"You have found it! You have found the way out!" screamed An-Tak. "Oh, Luata! And now I am too weak to go. Take me with you! Take me with you!"

"Shut up!" admonished Bradley. "You will have the whole flock of birds around our heads in a minute, and neither of us will escape. Be quiet, and I'll go ahead. If I find a way out, I'll come back and help you, if you'll promise not to try to eat me up again."

"I promise," cried An-Tak. "Oh, Luata! How could you blame me? I am half crazed of hunger and long confinement and the horror of the lizards and the rats and the constant waiting for death."

"I know," said Bradley simply. "I'm sorry for you, old top. Keep a stiff upper lip." And he slipped through the opening, found the ladder with his feet, closed the panel behind him, and started downward into the darkness.

Below him rose more and more distinctly the sound of running water. The air felt damp and cool. He could see nothing of his surroundings and felt nothing but the smooth, worn sides and rungs of the ladder down which he felt his way cautiously lest a broken rung or a misstep should hurl him downward.

As he descended thus slowly, the ladder seemed interminable and the pit bottomless, yet he realized when at last he reached the bottom that he could not have descended more than fifty feet. The bottom of the ladder rested on a narrow ledge paved with what felt like large round stones, but what he knew from experience to be human skulls. He could not but marvel as to where so many countless thousands of the things had come from, until he paused to consider that the infancy of Caspak dated doubtlessly back into remote ages, far beyond what the outer world considered the beginning of earthly time. For all these eons the Wieroos might have been collecting human skulls from their enemies and their own dead—enough to have built an entire city of them.

Feeling his way along the narrow ledge, Bradley came presently to a blank wall that stretched out over the water swirling beneath him, as far as he could reach. Stooping, he groped about with one hand, reaching down toward the surface of the water, and discovered that the bottom of the wall arched above the stream. How much space there was between the water and the arch he could not tell, nor how deep the former. There was only one way in which he might learn these things, and that was to lower himself into the stream. For only an instant he hesitated, weighing his chances. Behind him lay almost certainly the horrid fate of An-Tak; before him nothing worse than a comparatively painless death by drowning. Holding his haversack above his head with one hand he lowered his feet

78

slowly over the edge of the narrow platform. Almost immediately he felt the swirling of cold water about his ankles, and then with a silent prayer he let himself drop gently into the stream.

Great was Bradley's relief when he found the water no more than waist deep and beneath his feet a firm, gravel bottom. Feeling his way cautiously he moved downward with the current, which was not so strong as he had imagined from the noise of the running water.

Beneath the first arch he made his way, following the winding curvatures of the right-hand wall. After a few yards of progress his hand came suddenly in contact with a slimy thing clinging to the wall—a thing that hissed and scuttled out of reach. What it was, the man could not know; but almost instantly there was a splash in the water just ahead of him and then another.

On he went, passing beneath other arches at varying distances, and always in utter darkness. Unseen denizens of this great sewer, disturbed by the intruder, splashed into the water ahead of him and wriggled away. Time and again his hand touched them and never for an instant could he be sure that at the next step some gruesome thing might not attack him. He had strapped his haversack about his neck, well above the surface of the water, and in his left hand he carried his knife. Other precautions there were none to take.

The monotony of the blind trail was increased by the fact that from the moment he had started from the foot of the ladder he had counted his every step. He had promised to return for An-Tak if it proved humanly possible to do so, and he knew that in the blackness of the tunnel he could locate the foot of the ladder in no other way.

He had taken two hundred and sixty-nine steps—afterward he knew that he should never forget that number—when something bumped gently against him from behind. Instantly he wheeled about and with knife ready to defend himself stretched forth his right hand to push away the object that now had lodged against his body. His fingers feeling through the darkness came in contact with something cold and clammy—they passed to and fro over the thing until Bradley knew that it was the face of a dead man floating upon the surface of the stream. With an oath he pushed his gruesome companion out into mid-stream to float on down toward the great pool and the awaiting scavengers of the deep.

At his four hundred and thirteenth step another corpse bumped against him—how many had passed him without touching he could not guess; but suddenly he experienced the sensation of being surrounded by dead faces floating along with him, all set in hideous grimaces, their dead eyes glaring at this profaning alien who dared intrude upon the waters of this river of the dead—a horrid escort, pregnant with dire forebodings and with menace.

Though he advanced very slowly, he tried always to take steps of about the same length; so that he knew that though considerable time had elapsed, yet he had really advanced no more than four hundred yards when ahead he saw a lessening of the pitch-darkness, and at the next turn of the stream his surroundings became vaguely discernible. Above him was an arched roof and on either hand walls pierced at intervals by apertures covered with wooden doors. Just ahead of him in the roof of the aqueduct was a round, black hole about thirty inches in diameter. His eyes still rested upon the opening when there shot downward from it to the water below the naked body of a human being which almost immediately rose to the surface again and floated off down the stream. In the dim light Bradley saw that it was a dead Wieroo from which the wings and head had been removed. A moment later . another headless body floated past, recalling what An-Tak had told him of the skull-collecting customs of the Wieroo. Bradley wondered how it happened that the first corpse he had encountered in the stream had not been similarly mutilated.

The farther he advanced now, the lighter it became. The number of corpses was much smaller than he had imagined, only two more passing him before, at six hundred steps, or about five hundred yards, from the point he had taken to the stream, he came to the end of the tunnel and looked out upon sunlit water, running between grassy banks.

One of the last corpses to pass him was still clothed in the white robe of a Wieroo, blood-stained over the headless neck that it concealed.

Drawing closer to the opening leading into the bright daylight, Bradley surveyed what lay beyond. A short distance before him a large building stood in the center of several acres of grass and tree-covered ground, spanning the stream which disappeared through an opening in its foundation wall. From the large saucer-shaped roof and the vivid colorings of the various heterogeneous parts of the structure he recognized it as the temple past which he had been borne to the Blue Place of Seven Skulls.

To and fro flew Wieroos, going to and from the temple. Others passed on foot across the open grounds, assisting themselves with their great wings, so that they barely skimmed the earth. To leave the mouth of the tunnel would have been to court instant discovery and capture; but by what other avenue he might escape, Bradley could not guess, unless he retraced his steps up the stream and sought egress from the other end of the city. The thought of traversing that dark and horror-ridden tunnel for perhaps miles he could not entertain—there must be some other way. Perhaps after dark he could steal through the temple grounds and continue on downstream until he had come beyond the city; and so he stood and waited until his limbs became almost paralyzed with cold, and he knew that he must find some other plan for escape.

A half-formed decision to risk an attempt to swim under water to the temple was crystallizing in spite of the fact that any chance Wieroo flying above the stream might easily see him, when again a floating object bumped against him from behind and lodged across his back. Turning quickly he saw that the thing was what he had immediately guessed it to be—a headless and wingless Wieroo corpse. With a grunt of disgust he was about to push it from him when the white garment enshrouding it suggested a bold plan to his resourceful brain. Grasping the corpse by an arm he tore the garment from it and then let the body float downward toward the temple. With great care he draped the robe about him; the bloody blotch that had covered the severed neck he arranged about his own head. His haversack he rolled as tightly as possible and stuffed beneath his coat over his breast. Then he fell gently to the surface of the stream and lying upon his back floated downward with the current and out into the open sunlight.

Through the weave of the cloth he could distinguish large objects. He saw a Wieroo flap dismally above him; he saw the banks of the stream float slowly past; he heard a sudden wail upon the right—

hand shore, and his heart stood still lest his ruse had been discovered; but never by a move of a muscle did he betray that aught but a cold lump of clay floated there upon the bosom of the water, and soon, though it seemed an eternity to him, the direct sunlight was blotted out, and he knew that he had entered beneath the temple.

Quickly he felt for bottom with his feet and as quickly stood erect, snatching the bloody, clammy cloth from his face. On both sides were blank walls and before him the river turned a sharp corner and disappeared. Feeling his way cautiously forward he approached the turn and looked around the corner. To his left was a low platform about a foot above the level of the stream, and onto this he lost no time in climbing, for he was soaked from head to foot, cold and almost exhausted.

As he lay resting on the skull-paved shelf, he saw in the center of the vault above the river another of those sinister round holes through which he momentarily expected to see a headless corpse shoot downward in its last plunge to a watery grave. A few feet along the platform a closed door broke the blankness of the wall. As he lay looking at it and wondering what lay beyond, his mind filled with fragments of many wild schemes of escape, it opened and a white robed Wieroo stepped out upon the platform. The creature carried a large wooden basin filled with rubbish. Its eyes were not upon Bradley, who drew himself to a squatting position and crouched as far back in the corner of the niche in which the platform was set as he could force himself. The Wieroo stepped to the edge of the platform and dumped the rubbish into the stream. If it turned away from him as it started to retrace its steps to the doorway, there was a small chance that it might not see him; but if it turned toward him there was none at all. Bradley held his breath.

The Wieroo paused a moment, gazing down into the water, then it straightened up and turned toward the Englishman. Bradley did not move. The Wieroo stopped and stared intently at him. It approached him questioningly. Still Bradley remained as though carved of stone. The creature was directly in front of him. It stopped. There was no chance on earth that it would not discover what he was.

With the quickness of a cat, Bradley sprang to his feet and with all his great strength, backed by his heavy weight, struck the Wieroo upon the point of the chin. Without a sound the thing crumpled to the platform, while Bradley, acting almost instinctively to the urge of the first law of nature, rolled the inanimate body over the edge into the river.

Then he looked at the open doorway, crossed the platform and peered within the apartment beyond. What he saw was a large room, dimly lighted, and about the side rows of wooden vessels stacked one upon another. There was no Wieroo in sight, so the Englishman entered. At the far end of the room was another door, and as he crossed toward it, he glanced into some of the vessels, which he found were filled with dried fruits, vegetables and fish. Without more ado he stuffed his pockets and his haversack full, thinking of the poor creature awaiting his return in the gloom of the Place of Seven Skulls.

When night came, he would return and fetch An-Tak this far at least; but in the meantime it was his intention to reconnoiter in the hope that he might discover some easier way out of the city than that offered by the chill, black channel of the ghastly river of corpses.

Beyond the farther door stretched a long passageway from which closed doorways led into other parts of the cellars of the temple. A few yards from the storeroom a ladder rose from the corridor through an aperture in the ceiling. Bradley paused at the foot of it, debating the wisdom of further investigation against a return to the river; but strong within him was the spirit of exploration that has scattered his race to the four corners of the earth. What new mysteries lay hidden in the chambers above? The urge to know was strong upon him though his better judgment warned him that the safer course lay in retreat. For a moment he stood thus, running his fingers through his hair; then he cast discretion to the winds and began the ascent.

In conformity with such Wieroo architecture as he had already observed, the well through which the ladder rose continually canted at an angle from the perpendicular. At more or less regular stages it was pierced by apertures closed by doors, none of which he could open until he had climbed fully fifty feet from the river level. Here he discovered a door already ajar opening into a large, circular chamber, the walls and floors of which were covered with the skins of wild beasts and with rugs of many colors; but what interested him most was the occupants of the room—a Wieroo, and a girl of human proportions. She was standing with her back against a column which rose from the center of the apartment from floor to ceiling—a hollow column about forty inches in diameter in which he could see an opening some thirty inches across. The girl's side was toward Bradley, and her face averted, for she was watching the Wieroo, who was now advancing slowly toward her, talking as he came.

Bradley could distinctly hear the words of the creature, who was urging the girl to accompany him to another Wieroo city. "Come with me," he said, "and you shall have your life; remain here and He Who Speaks for Luata will claim you for his own; and when he is done with you, your skull will bleach at the top of a tall staff while your body feeds the reptiles at the mouth of the River of Death. Even though you bring into the world a female Wieroo, your fate will be the same if you do not escape him, while with me you shall have life and food and none shall harm you."

He was quite close to the girl when she replied by striking him in the face with all her strength. "Until I am slain," she cried, "I shall fight against you all." From the throat of the Wieroo issued that dismal wail that Bradley had heard so often in the past—it was like a scream of pain smothered to a groan— and then the thing leaped upon the girl, its face working in hideous grimaces as it clawed and beat at her to force her to the floor.

The Englishman was upon the point of entering to defend her when a door at the opposite side of the chamber opened to admit a huge Wieroo clothed entirely in red. At sight of the two struggling upon the floor the newcomer raised his voice in a shriek of rage. Instantly the Wieroo who was attacking the girl leaped to his feet and faced the other.

"I heard," screamed he who had just entered the room. "I heard, and when He Who Speaks for Luata shall have heard—" He paused and made a suggestive movement of a finger across his throat.

"He shall not hear," returned the first Wieroo as, with a powerful motion of his great wings, he launched himself upon the red-robed figure. The latter dodged the first charge, drew a wicked-looking, curved blade from beneath its red robe, spread its wings and dived for its antagonist. Beating their wings, wailing and groaning, the two hideous things sparred for position. The white-robed one being un-armed sought to grasp the other by the wrist of its knife-hand and by the throat, while the latter hopped around on its dainty white feet, seeking an opening for a mortal blow. Once it struck and missed, and then the other rushed in and clinched, at the same time securing both the holds it sought. Immediately the two commenced beating at each other's heads with the joints of their wings, kicking with their soft, puny feet and biting, each at the other's face.

In the meantime the girl moved about the room, keeping out of the way of the duelists, and as she did so, Bradley caught a glimpse of her full face and immediately recognized her as the girl of the place of the yellow door. He did not dare intervene now until one of the Wieroo had overcome the other, lest the two should turn upon him at once, when the chances were fair that he would be defeated in so unequal a battle as the curved blade of the red Wieroo would render it, and so he waited, watching the white-robed figure slowly choking the life from him of the red robe. The protruding tongue and the popping eyes proclaimed that the end was near and a moment later the red robe sank to the floor of the room, the curved blade slipping from nerveless fingers. For an instant longer the victor clung to the throat of his defeated antagonist and then he rose, dragging the body after him, and approached the central column. Here he raised the body and thrust it into the aperture where Bradley saw it drop suddenly from sight. Instantly there flashed into his memory the circular openings in the roof of the river vault and the corpses he had seen drop from them to the water beneath.

As the body disappeared, the Wieroo turned and cast about the room for the girl. For a moment he stood eying her. "You saw," he muttered, "and if you tell them, He Who Speaks for Luata will have my wings severed while still I live and my head will be severed and I shall be cast into the River of Death, for thus it happens even to the highest who slay one of the red robe. You saw, and you must die!" he ended with a scream as he rushed upon the girl.

Bradley waited no longer. Leaping into the room he ran for the Wieroo, who had already seized the girl, and as he ran, he stooped and picked up the curved blade. The creature's back was toward him as, with his left hand, he seized it by the neck. Like a flash the great wings beat backward as the creature turned, and Bradley was swept from his feet, though he still retained his hold upon the blade. Instantly the Wieroo was upon him. Bradley lay slightly raised upon his left elbow, his right arm free, and as the thing came close, he cut at the hideous face with all the strength that lay within him. The blade struck at the junction of the neck and torso and with such force as to completely decapitate the Wieroo, the hideous head dropping to the floor and the body falling forward upon the Englishman. Pushing it from him he rose to his feet and faced the wide-eyed girl.

"Luata!" she exclaimed. "How came you here?"

Bradley shrugged. "Here I am," he said; "but the thing now is to get out of here—both of us."

The girl shook her head. "It cannot be," she stated sadly.

"That is what I thought when they dropped me

nto the Blue Place of Seven Skulls," replied Bradey. "Can't be done. I did it. —Here! You're mussing up the floor something awful, you." This last to the lead Wieroo as he stooped and dragged the corpse o the central shaft, where he raised it to the aperure and let it slip into the tube. Then he picked up he head and tossed it after the body. "Don't be so glum," he admonished the former as he carried it toward the well; "smile!"

"But how can he smile?" questioned the girl, a half-puzzled, half-frightened look upon her face. "He is dead."

"That's so," admitted Bradley, "and I suppose he does feel a bit cut up about it."

The girl shook her head and edged away from the man—toward the door.

"Come!" said the Englishman. "We've got to get out of here. If you don't know a better way than the river, it's the river then."

The girl still eyed him askance. "But how could he smile when he was dead?"

Bradley laughed aloud. "I thought we English were supposed to have the least sense of humor of any people in the world," he cried; "but now I've found one human being who hasn't any. Of course you don't know half I'm saying; but don't worry, little girl; I'm not going to hurt you, and if I can get you out of here, I'll do it."

Even if she did not understand all he said, she at least read something in his smiling countenance—something which reassured her. "I do not fear you," she said; "though I do not understand all that you say even though you speak my own tongue and use words that I know. But as for escaping"—she sighed—"alas, how can it be done?"

"I escaped from the Blue Place of Seven Skulls,"

Bradley reminded her. "Come!" And he turned toward the shaft and the ladder that he had ascended from the river. "We cannot waste time here."

The girl followed him; but at the doorway both drew back, for from below came the sound of some one ascending.

Bradley tiptoed to the door and peered cautiously into the well; then he stepped back beside the girl. "There are half a dozen of them coming up; but possibly they will pass this room."

"No," she said, "they will pass directly through this room—they are on their way to Him Who Speaks for Luata. We may be able to hide in the next room—there are skins there beneath which we may crawl. They will not stop in that room; but they may stop in this one for a short time—the other room is blue."

"What's that got to do with it?" demanded the Englishman.

"They fear blue," she replied. "In every room where murder has been done you will find blue—a certain amount for each murder. When the room is all blue, they shun it. This room has much blue; but evidently they kill mostly in the next room, which is now all blue."

"But there is blue on the outside of every house I have seen," said Bradley.

"Yes," assented the girl, "and there are blue rooms in each of those houses—when all the rooms are blue then the whole outside of the house will be blue as is the Blue Place of Seven Skulls. There are many such here."

"And the skulls with blue upon them?" inquired Bradley. "Did they belong to murderers?"

"They were murdered—some of them; those with only a small amount of blue were murderers—

nown murderers. All Wieroos are murderers. When
hey have committed a certain number of murders
vithout being caught at it, they confess to Him Who
peaks for Luata and are advanced, after which
hey wear robes with a slash of some color—I think
ellow comes first. When they reach a point where
heir entire robe is of yellow, they discard it for a
vhite robe with a red slash; and when one wins a
omplete red robe, he carries such a long, curved
nife as you have in your hand; after that comes the
lue slash on a white robe, and then, I suppose, an
ll blue robe. I have never seen such a one."

As they talked in low tones they had moved from
he room of the death shaft into an all blue room ad-
oining, where they sat down together in a corner
vith their backs against a wall and drew a pile of
ides over themselves. A moment later they heard a
umber of Wieroos enter the chamber. They were
alking together as they crossed the floor, or the two
ould not have heard them. Halfway across the
hamber they halted as the door toward which they
vere advancing opened and a dozen others of their
ind entered the apartment.

Bradley could guess all this by the increased vol-
me of sound and the dismal greetings; but the sud-
len silence that almost immediately ensued he
ould not fathom, for he could not know that from
eneath one of the hides that covered him protrud-
d one of his heavy army shoes, or that some eigh-
een large Wieroos with robes either solid red or
lashed with red or blue were standing gazing at it.
Nor could he hear their stealthy approach.

The first intimation he had that he had been dis-
overed was when his foot was suddenly seized, and
e was yanked violently from beneath the hides to
nd himself surrounded by menacing blades. They

would have slain him on the spot had not one clothed all in red held them back, saying that He Who Speaks for Luata desired to see this strange creature.

As they led Bradley away, he caught an opportunity to glance back toward the hides to see what had become of the girl, and, to his gratification, he discovered that she still lay concealed beneath the hides. He wondered if she would have the nerve to attempt the river trip alone and regretted that now he could not accompany her. He felt rather all in himself, more so than he had at any time since he had been captured by the Wieroo, for there appeared not the slightest cause for hope in his present predicament. He had dropped the curved blade beneath the hides when he had been jerked so violently from their fancied security. It was almost in a spirit of resigned hopelessness that he quietly accompanied his captors through various chambers and corridors toward the heart of the temple.

CHAPTER FOUR

THE FARTHER the group progressed, the more barbaric and the more sumptuous became the decorations. Hides of leopard and tiger predominated, apparently because of their more beautiful markings, and decorative skulls became more and more numerous. Many of the latter were mounted in precious metals and set with colored stones and priceless gems, while thick upon the hides that covered the walls were golden ornaments similar to those worn by the girl and those which had filled the chests he had examined in the storeroom of Foshbal-soj, leading the Englishman to the conviction that all such were spoils of war or theft, since each piece seemed made for personal adornment, while in so far as he had seen, no Wieroo wore ornaments of any sort.

And also as they advanced the more numerous became the Wieroos moving hither and thither within the temple. Many now were the solid red robes and those that were slashed with blue—a veritable hive of murderers.

At last the party halted in a room in which were many Wieroos who gathered about Bradley questioning his captors and examining him and his apparel. One of the party accompanying the Englishman spoke to a Wieroo that stood beside a door leading from the room. "Tell Him Who Speaks for Luata," he said, "that Fosh-bal-soj we could not find; but that in returning we found this creature within the temple, hiding. It must be the same that Fosh-bal-soj captured in the Sto-lu country during the last darkness. Doubtless He Who Speaks for Luata would wish to see and question this strange thing."

The creature addressed turned and slipped through the doorway, closing the door after it, but first depositing its curved blade upon the floor without. Its post was immediately taken by another, and Bradley now saw that at least twenty such guards loitered in the immediate vicinity. The doorkeeper was gone but for a moment, and when he returned, he signified that Bradley's party was to enter the next chamber; but first each of the Wieroos removed his curved weapon and laid it upon the floor. The door was swung open, and the party, now reduced to Bradley and five Wieroos, was ushered across the threshold into a large, irregularly shaped room in which a single, giant Wieroo whose robe was solid blue sat upon a raised dais.

The creature's face was white with the whiteness of a corpse, its dead eyes entirely expressionless, its cruel, thin lips tight-drawn against yellow teeth in a perpetual grimace. Upon either side of it lay an enormous, curved sword, similar to those with which some of the other Wieroos had been armed, but larger and heavier. Constantly its clawlike fingers played with one or the other of these weapons.

The walls of the chamber as well as the floor were entirely hidden by skins and woven fabrics. Blue predominated in all the colorations. Fastened against the hides were many pairs of Wieroo wings, mounted so that they resembled long, black shields. Upon the ceiling were painted in blue characters a bewildering series of hieroglyphics and upon pedestals set against the walls or standing out well within the room were many human skulls.

As the Wieroos approached the figure upon the dais, they leaned far forward, raising their wings above their heads and stretching their necks as though offering them to the sharp swords of the grim and hideous creature.

"O Thou Who Speakest for Luata!" exclaimed one of the party. "We bring you the strange creature that Fosh-bal-soj captured and brought thither at thy command."

So this then was the godlike figure that spoke for divinity! This arch-murderer was the Caspakian representative of God on Earth! His blue robe announced him the one and the seeming humility of his minions the other. For a long minute he glared at Bradley. Then he began to question him—from whence he came and how, the name and description of his native country, and a hundred other queries.

"Are you *cos-ata-lu?*" the creature asked.

Bradley replied that he was and that all his kind were, as well as every living thing in his part of the world.

"Can you tell me the secret?" asked the creature.

Bradley hesitated and then, thinking to gain time, replied in the affirmative.

"What is it?" demanded the Wieroo, leaning far forward and exhibiting every evidence of excited interest.

Bradley leaned forward and whispered: "It is for your ears alone; I will not divulge it to others, and then only on condition that you carry me and the girl I saw in the place of the yellow door near to that of Fosh-bal-soj back to her own country."

The thing rose in wrath, holding one of its swords above its head.

"Who are you to make terms for Him Who Speaks for Luata?" it shrilled. "Tell me the secret or die where you stand!"

"And if I die now, the secret goes with me," Bradley reminded him. "Never again will you get the opportunity to question another of my kind who knows the secret." Anything to gain time, to get the rest of the Wieroos from the room, that he might plan some scheme for escape and put it into effect.

The creature turned upon the leader of the party that had brought Bradley.

"Is the thing with weapons?" it asked.

"No," was the response.

"Then go; but tell the guard to remain close by," commanded the high one.

The Wieroos salaamed and withdrew, closing the door behind them. He Who Speaks for Luata grasped a sword nervously in his right hand. At his left side lay the second weapon. It was evident that he lived in constant dread of being assassinated. The fact that he permitted none with weapons within his presence and that he always kept two swords at his side pointed to this.

Bradley was racking his brain to find some suggestion of a plan whereby he might turn the situation to his own account. His eyes wandered past the weird figure before him; they played about the walls of the apartment as though hoping to draw inspiration from the dead skulls and the hides and the wings, and then they came back to the face of the Wieroo god, now working in anger.

"Quick!" screamed the thing. "The secret!"

"Will you give me and the girl our freedom?" insisted Bradley.

For an instant the thing hesitated, and then it grumbled "Yes." At the same instant Bradley saw two hides upon the wall directly back of the dais separate and a face appear in the opening. No change of expression upon the Englishman's countenance betrayed that he had seen aught to surprise him, though surprised he was for the face in the aperture was that of the girl he had but just left hidden beneath the hides in another chamber. A white and shapely arm now pushed past the face into the room, and in the hand, tightly clutched, was the curved blade, smeared with blood, that Bradley had dropped beneath the hides at the moment he had been discovered and drawn from his concealment.

"Listen, then," said Bradley in a low voice to the Wieroo. "You shall know the secret of *cos-ata-lu* as well as do I; but none other may hear it. Lean close —I will whisper it into your ear."

He moved forward and stepped upon the dais. The creature raised its sword ready to strike at the first indication of treachery, and Bradley stooped beneath the blade and put his ear close to the gruesome face. As he did so, he rested his weight upon his hands, one upon either side of the Wieroo's body, his right hand upon the hilt of the spare sword lying at the left of Him Who Speaks for Luata.

"This then is the secret of both life and death," he whispered, and at the same instant he grasped the Wieroo by the right wrist and with his own right hand swung the extra blade in a sudden vicious blow against the creature's neck before the thing could give even a single cry of alarm; then without waiting an instant Bradley leaped past the dead god and vanished behind the hides that had hidden the girl.

Wide-eyed and panting the girl seized his arm. "Oh, what have you done?" she cried. "He Who Speaks for Luata will be avenged by Luata. Now indeed must you die. There is no escape, for even though we reached my own country Luata can find you out."

"Bosh!" exclaimed Bradley, and then: "But you were going to knife him yourself."

"Then I alone should have died," she replied.

Bradley scratched his head. "Neither of us is going to die," he said; "at least not at the hands of any god. If we don't get out of here though, we'll die right enough. Can you find your way back to the room where I first came upon you in the temple?"

"I know the way," replied the girl; "but I doubt if we can go back without being seen. I came hither because I only met Wieroos who knew that I am supposed now to be in the temple; but you could go elsewhere without being discovered."

Bradley's ingenuity had come up against a stone wall. There seemed no possibility of escape. He looked about him. They were in a small room where lay a litter of rubbish—torn bits of cloth, old hides, pieces of fiber rope. In the center of the room was a cylindrical shaft with an opening in its face. Bradley knew it for what it was. Here the arch-fiend dragged his victims and cast their bodies into the river of death far below. The floor about the opening in the shaft and the sides of the shaft were clotted thick with a dried, dark brown substance that the Englishman knew had once been blood. The place had the appearance of having been a veritable shambles. An odor of decaying flesh permeated the air.

The Englishman crossed to the shaft and peered into the opening. All below was dark as pitch; but at the bottom he knew was the river. Suddenly an inspiration and a bold scheme leaped to his mind. Turning quickly he hunted about the room until he found what he sought—a quantity of the rope that lay strewn here and there. With rapid fingers he unsnarled the different lengths, the girl helping him, and then he tied the ends together until he had three ropes about seventy-five feet in length. He fastened these together at each end and without a word secured one of the ends about the girl's body beneath her arms.

"Don't be frightened," he said at length, as he led her toward the opening in the shaft. "I'm going to lower you to the river, and then I'm coming down after you. When you are safe below, give two quick jerks upon the rope. If there is danger there and you want me to draw you up into the shaft, jerk once. Don't be afraid—it is the only way."

"I am not afraid," replied the girl, rather haughtily Bradley thought, and herself climbed through the aperture and hung by her hands waiting for Bradley to lower her.

As rapidly as was consistent with safety, the man paid out the rope. When it was about half out, he heard loud cries and wails suddenly arise within the room they had just quitted. The slaying of their god had been discovered by the Wieroos. A search for the slayer would begin at once.

Lord! Would the girl never reach the river? At last, just as he was positive that searchers were already entering the room behind him, there came two quick tugs at the rope. Instantly Bradley made the rest of the strands fast about the shaft, slipped into the black tube and began a hurried descent toward the river. An instant later he stood waist deep in water beside the girl. Impulsively she reached toward him and grasped his arm. A strange thrill ran through him at the contact; but he only cut the rope from about her body and lifted her to the little shelf at the river's side.

"How can we leave here?" she asked.

"By the river," he replied; "but first I must go back to the Blue Place of Seven Skulls and get the poor devil I left there. I'll have to wait until after dark, though, as I cannot pass through the open stretch of river in the temple gardens by day."

"There is another way," said the girl. "I have never seen it; but often I have heard them speak of it—a corridor that runs beside the river from one end of the city to the other. Through the gardens it is below ground. If we could find an entrance to it, we could leave here at once. It is not safe here, for they will search every inch of the temple and the grounds."

"Come," said Bradley. "We'll have a look for it, anyway." And so saying he approached one of the doors that opened onto the skull-paved shelf.

They found the corridor easily, for it paralleled the river, separated from it only by a single wall. It took them beneath the gardens and the city, always through inky darkness. After they had reached the other side of the gardens, Bradley counted his steps until he had retraced as many as he had taken coming down the stream; but though they had to grope their way along, it was a much more rapid trip than the former.

When he thought he was about opposite the point at which he had descended from the Blue Place of Seven Skulls, he sought and found a doorway lead-

ing out onto the river; and then, still in the blackest
darkness, he lowered himself into the stream and
felt up and down upon the opposite side for the little shelf and the ladder. Ten yards from where he
had emerged he found them, while the girl waited
upon the opposite side.

To ascend to the secret panel was the work of but
a minute. Here he paused and listened lest a Wieroo
might be visiting the prison in search of him or the
other inmate; but no sound came from the gloomy
interior. Bradley could not but muse upon the joy of
the man on the opposite side when he should drop
down to him with food and a new hope for escape.
Then he opened the panel and looked into the room.
The faint light from the grating above revealed the
pile of rags in one corner; but the man lay beneath
them, he made no response to Bradley's low greeting.

The Englishman lowered himself to the floor of
the room and approached the rags. Stooping he lifted a corner of them. Yes, there was the man asleep.
Bradley shook him—there was no response. He
stooped lower and in the dim light examined An-
Tak; then he stood up with a sigh. A rat leaped from
beneath the coverings and scurried away. "Poor
devil!" muttered Bradley.

He crossed the room to swing himself to the perch
preparatory to quitting the Blue Place of Seven
Skulls forever. Beneath the perch he paused. "I'll
not give them the satisfaction," he growled. "Let
them believe that he escaped."

Returning to the pile of rags he gathered the man
into his arms. It was difficult work raising him to the
high perch and dragging him through the small
opening and thus down the ladder; but presently it

was done, and Bradley had lowered the body into the river and cast it off. "Good-bye, old top!" he whispered.

A moment later he had rejoined the girl and hand in hand they were following the dark corridor upstream toward the farther end of the city. She told him that the Wieroos seldom frequented these lower passages, as the air here was too chill for them; but occasionally they came, and as they could see quite as well by night as by day, they would be sure to discover Bradley and the girl.

"If they come close enough," she said, "we can see their eyes shining in the dark—they resemble dull splotches of light. They glow, but do not blaze like the eyes of the tiger or the lion."

The man could not but note the very evident horror with which she mentioned the creatures. To him they were uncanny; but she had been used to them for a year almost, and probably all her life she had either seen or heard of them constantly.

"Why do you fear them so?" he asked. "It seems more than any ordinary fear of the harm they can do you."

She tried to explain; but the nearest he could gather was that she looked upon the Wieroo almost as supernatural beings. "There is a legend current among my people that once the Wieroo were unlike us only in that they possessed rudimentary wings. They lived in villages in the Galu country, and while the two peoples often warred, they held no hatred for one another. In those days each race came up from the beginning and there was great rivalry as to which was the higher in the scale of evolution. The Wieroo developed the first *cos-ata-lu;* but they were always male—never could they reproduce woman. Slowly they commenced to develop certain attri-

104

butes of the mind which, they considered, placed them upon a still higher level and which gave them many advantages over us, seeing which they thought only of mental development—their minds became like the stars and the rivers, moving always in the same manner, never varying. They called this *tas-ad*, which means doing everything the right way, or, in other words, the Wieroo way. If foe or friend, right or wrong, stood in the way of *tas-ad*, then it must be crushed.

"Soon the Galus and the lesser races of men came to hate and fear them. It was then that the Wieroos decided to carry *tas-ad* into every part of the world. They were very warlike and very numerous, although they had long since adopted the policy of slaying all those among them whose wings did not show advanced development.

"It took ages for all this to happen—very slowly came the different changes; but at last the Wieroos had wings they could use. But by reason of always making war upon their neighbors they were hated by every creature of Caspak, for no one wanted their *tas-ad*, and so they used their wings to fly to this island when the other races turned against them and threatened to kill them all. So cruel had they become and so bloodthirsty that they no longer had hearts that beat with love or sympathy; but their very cruelty and wickedness kept them from conquering the other races, since they were also cruel and wicked to one another, so that no Wieroo trusted another.

"Always were they slaying those above them that they might rise in power and possessions, until at last came the more powerful than the others with a *tas-ad* all his own. He gathered about him a few of the most terrible Wieroos, and among them they made laws which took from all but these few Wieroos every weapon they possessed.

"Now their *tas-ad* has reached a high plane among them. They make many wonderful things that we cannot make. They think great thoughts, no doubt, and still dream of greatness to come, but their thoughts and their acts are regulated by ages of custom—they are all alike—and they are most unhappy."

As the girl talked, the two moved steadily along the dark passageway beside the river. They had advanced a considerable distance when there sounded faintly from far ahead the muffled roar of falling water, which increased in volume as they moved forward until at last it filled the corridor with a deafening sound. Then the corridor ended in a blank wall; but in a niche to the right was a ladder leading aloft, and to the left was a door opening onto the river. Bradley tried the latter first and as he opened it, felt a heavy spray against his face. The little shelf outside the doorway was wet and slippery, the roaring of the water tremendous. There could be but one explanation—they had reached a waterfall in the river, and if the corridor actually terminated here, their escape was effectually cut off, since it was quite evidently impossible to follow the bed of the river and ascend the falls.

As the ladder was the only alternative, the two turned toward it and, the man first, began the ascent, which was through a well similar to that which had led him to the upper floors of the temple. As he climbed, Bradley felt for openings in the sides of the shaft; but he discovered none below fifty feet. The first he came to was ajar, letting a faint light into the well. As he paused, the girl climbed to his

de, and together they looked through the crack
ito a low-ceiled chamber in which were several
:alu women and an equal number of hideous little
:plicas of the full-grown Wieroos with which Brad-
·y was not quite familiar.

He could feel the body of the girl pressed close to
is tremble as her eyes rested upon the inmates of
1e room, and involuntarily his arm encircled her
1oulders as though to protect her from some
anger which he sensed without recognizing.

"Poor things," she whispered. "This is their horri-
le fate—to be imprisoned here beneath the surface
f the city with their hideous offspring whom they
ate as they hate their fathers. A Wieroo keeps his
1ildren thus hidden until they are full-grown lest
1ey be murdered by their fellows. The lower rooms
f the city are filled with many such as these."

Several feet above was a second door beyond
·hich they found a small room stored with food in
·ooden vessels. A grated window in one wall
pened above an alley, and through it they could
:e that they were just below the roof of the build-
1g. Darkness was coming, and at Bradley's sugges-
on they decided to remain hidden here until after
ark and then to ascend to the roof and reconnoiter.

Shortly after they had settled themselves they
eard something descending the ladder from above.
'hey hoped that it would continue on down the
·ell and fairly held their breath as the sound ap-
roaching the door to the storeroom. Their hearts
ınk as they heard the door open and from between
racks in the vessels behind which they hid saw a
ellow-slashed Wieroo enter the room. Each recog-
ized him immediately, the girl indicating the fact
f her own recognition by a sudden pressure of her

fingers on Bradley's arm. It was the Wieroo of the yellow slashing whose abode was the place of the yellow door in which Bradley had first seen the girl.

The creature carried a wooden bowl which was filled with dried food from several of the vessels; then it turned and quit the room. Bradley could see through the partially open doorway that it descended the ladder. The girl told him that it was taking the food to the women and the young below, and that while it might return immediately, the chances were that it would remain for some time.

"We are just below the place of the yellow door," she said. "It is far from the edge of the city; so far that we may not hope to escape if we ascend to the roofs here."

"I think," replied the man, "that of all the places in Oo-oh this will be the easiest to escape from. Anyway, I want to return to the place of the yellow door and get my pistol if it is there."

"It is still there," replied the girl. "I saw it placed in a chest where he keeps the things he takes from his prisoners and victims."

"Good!" exclaimed Bradley. "Now come, quickly." And the two crossed the room to the well and ascended the ladder a short distance to its top where they found another door that opened into a vacant room—the same in which Bradley had first met the girl. To find the pistol was a matter of but a moment's search on the part of Bradley's companion and then, at the Englishman's signal, she followed him to the yellow door.

It was quite dark without as the two entered the narrow passage between two buildings. A few steps brought them undiscovered to the doorway of the storeroom where lay the body of Fosh-bal-soj. In the distance, toward the temple, they could hear sounds as of a great gathering of Wieroos—the peculiar, uncanny wailing rising above the dismal flapping of countless wings.

"They have heard of the killing of Him Who Speaks for Luata," whispered the girl. "Soon they will spread in all directions searching for us."

"And will they find us?"

"As surely as Lua gives light by day," she replied; "and when they find us, they will tear us to pieces, for only the Wieroos may murder—only they may practice *tas-ad*."

"But they will not kill you," said Bradley. "You did not slay him."

"It will make no difference," she insisted. "If they find us together they will slay us both."

"Then they won't find us together," announced Bradley decisively. "You stay right here—you won't be any worse off than before I came—and I'll get as far as I can and account for as many of the beggers as possible before they get me. Good-bye! You're a mighty decent little girl. I wish that I might have helped you."

"No," she cried. "Do not leave me. I would rather die. I had hoped and hoped to find some way to return to my own country. I wanted to go back to An-Tak, who must be very lonely without me; but I know that it can never be. It is difficult to kill hope, though mine is nearly dead. Do not leave me."

"An-Tak!" Bradley repeated. "You loved a man called An-Tak?"

"Yes," replied the girl. "An-Tak was away, hunting, when the Wieroo caught me. How he must have grieved for me! He also was *cos-ata-lu*, twelve moons older than I, and all our lives we have been together."

Bradley remained silent. So she loved An-Tak. He

hadn't the heart to tell her that An-Tak had died, or how.

At the door of Fosh-bal-soj's storeroom they halted to listen. No sound came from within, and gently Bradley pushed open the door. All was inky darkness as they entered; but presently their eyes became accustomed to the gloom that was partially relieved by the soft starlight without. The Englishman searched and found those things for which he had come—two robes, two pairs of dead wings and several lengths of fiber rope. One pair of the wings he adjusted to the girl's shoulders by means of the rope. Then he draped the robe about her, carrying the cowl over her head.

He heard her gasp of astonishment when she realized the ingenuity and boldness of his plan; then he directed her to adjust the other pair of wings and the robe upon him. Working with strong, deft fingers she soon had the work completed, and the two stepped out upon the roof, to all intent and purpose genuine Wieroos. Besides his pistol Bradley carried the sword of the slain Wieroo prophet, while the girl was armed with the small blade of the red Wieroo.

Side by side they walked slowly across the roofs toward the north edge of the city. Wieroos flapped above them and several times they passed others walking or sitting upon the roofs. From the temple still rose the sounds of commotion, now pierced by occasional shrill screams.

"The murderers are abroad," whispered the girl. "Thus will another become the tongue of Luata. It is well for us, since it keeps them too busy to give the time for searching for us. They think that we cannot escape the city, and they know that we cannot leave the island—and so do I."

Bradley shook his head. "If there is any way, we will find it," he said.

"There is no way," replied the girl.

Bradley made no response, and in silence they continued until the outer edge of roofs was visible before them. "We are almost there," he whispered.

The girl felt for his fingers and pressed them. He could feel hers trembling as he returned the pressure, nor did he relinquish her hand; and thus they came to the edge of the last roof.

Here they halted and looked about them. To be seen attempting to descend to the ground below would be to betray the fact that they were not Wieroos. Bradley wished that their wings were attached to their bodies by sinew and muscle rather than by ropes of fiber. A Wieroo was flapping far overhead. Two more stood near a door a few yards distant. Standing between these and one of the outer pedestals that supported one of the numerous skulls Bradley made one end of a piece of rope fast about the pedestal and dropped the other end to the ground outside the city. Then they waited.

It was an hour before the coast was entirely clear and then a moment came when no Wieroo was in sight. "Now!" whispered Bradley; and the girl grasped the rope and slid over the edge of the roof into the darkness below. A moment later Bradley felt two quick pulls upon the rope and immediately followed to the girl's side.

Across a narrow clearing they made their way and into a wood beyond. All night they walked, following the river upward toward its source, and at dawn they took shelter in a thicket beside the stream. At no time did they hear the cry of a carnivore, and though many startled animals fled as they approached, they were not once menaced by a wild beast. When Bradley expressed surprise at the absence of the fiercest beasts that are so numerous upon the mainland of Caprona, the girl explained the reason that is contained in one of their ancient legends.

"When the Wieroos first developed wings upon which they could fly, they found this island devoid of any life other than a few reptiles that live either upon land or in the water and these only close to the coast. Requiring meat for food the Wieroos carried to the island such animals as they wished for that purpose. They still occasionally bring them, and this with the natural increase keeps them provided with flesh."

"As it will us," suggested Bradley.

The first day they remained in hiding, eating only the dried food that Bradley had brought with him from the temple storeroom, and the next night they set out again up the river, continuing steadily on until almost dawn, when they came to low hills where the river wound through a gorge—it was little more than rivulet now, the water clear and cold and filled with fish similar to brook trout though much larger. Not wishing to leave the stream the two waded along its bed to a spot where the gorge widened between perpendicular bluffs to a wooded acre of level land. Here they stopped, for here also the stream ended. They had reached its source— many cold springs bubbling up from the center of a little natural amphitheater in the hills and forming a clear and beautiful pool overshadowed by trees upon one side and bounded by a little clearing upon the other.

With the coming of the sun they saw they had stumbled upon a place where they might remain hidden from the Wieroos for a long time and also one that they could defend against these winged creatures, since the trees would shield them from an attack from above and also hamper the movements of the creatures should they attempt to follow them into the wood.

For three days they rested here before trying to explore the neighboring country. On the fourth, Bradley stated that he was going to scale the bluffs and learn what lay beyond. He told the girl that she should remain in hiding; but she refused to be left, saying that whatever fate was to be his, she intended to share it, so that he was at last forced to permit her to come with him. Through woods at the summit of the bluff they made their way toward the north and had gone but a short distance when the wood ended and before them they saw the waters of the inland sea and dimly in the distance the coveted shore.

The beach lay some two hundred yards from the foot of the hill on which they stood, nor was there a tree nor any other form of shelter between them and the water as far up and down the coast as they could see. Among other plans Bradley had thought of constructing a covered raft upon which they might drift to the mainland; but as such a contrivance would necessarily be of considerable weight, it must be built in the water of the sea, since they could not hope to move it even a short distance overland.

"If this wood was only at the edge of the water," he sighed.

"But it is not," the girl reminded him, and then: "Let us make the best of it. We have escaped from death for a time at least. We have food and good water and peace and each other. What more could we have upon the mainland?"

"But I thought you wanted to get back to your own country!" he exclaimed.

She cast her eyes upon the ground and half turned away. "I do," she said, "yet I am happy here. I could be little happier there."

Bradley stood in silent thought. "'We have food and good water and peace and *each other!'*" he repeated to himself. He turned then and looked at the girl, and it was as though in the days that they had been together this was the first time that he had really seen her. The circumstances that had thrown them together, the dangers through which they had passed, all the weird and horrible surroundings that had formed the background of his knowledge of her had had their effect—she had been but the companion of an adventure; her self-reliance, her endurance, her loyalty, had been only what one man might expect of another, and he saw that he had unconsciously assumed an attitude toward her that he might have assumed toward a man. Yet there had been a difference—he recalled now the strange sensation of elation that had thrilled him upon the occasions when the girl had pressed his hand in hers, and the depression that had followed her announcement of her love for An-Tak.

He took a step toward her. A fierce yearning to seize her and crush her in his arms, swept over him, and then there flashed upon the screen of recollection the picture of a stately hall set amidst broad gardens and ancient trees and of a proud old man with beetling brows—an old man who held his head very high—and Bradley shook his head and turned away again.

They went back then to their little acre, and the days came and went, and the man fashioned spear and bow and arrows and hunted with them that they might have meat, and he made hooks of fish-bone and caught fishes with wondrous flies of his own invention; and the girl gathered fruits and cooked the flesh and the fish and made beds of branches and soft grasses. She cured the hides of the animals he killed and made them soft by much pounding. She made sandals for herself and for the man and fashioned a hide after the manner of those worn by the warriors of her tribe and made the man wear it, for his own garments were in rags.

She was always the same—sweet and kind and helpful—but always there was about her manner and her expression just a trace of wistfulness, and often she sat and looked at the man when he did not know it, her brows puckered in thought as though she were trying to fathom and to understand him.

In the face of the cliff, Bradley scooped a cave from the rotted granite of which the hill was composed, making a shelter for them against the rains. He brought wood for their cook-fire which they used only in the middle of the day—a time when there was little likelihood of Wieroos being in the air so far from their city—and then he learned to bank it with earth in such a way that the embers held until the following noon without giving off smoke.

Always he was planning on reaching the mainland, and never a day passed that he did not go to the top of the hill and look out across the sea toward the dark, distant line that meant for him comparative freedom and possibly reunion with his comrades. The girl always went with him, standing at his side and watching the stern expression on his face with just a tinge of sadness on her own.

"You're not happy," she said once.

"I should be over there with my men," he replied. "I do not know what may have happened to them."

"I want you to be happy," she said quite simply; "but I should be very lonely if you went away and left me here."

He put his hand on her shoulder. "I would not do that, little girl," he said gently. "If you cannot go with me, I shall not go. If either of us must go alone, it will be you."

Her face lighted to a wondrous smile. "Then we shall not be separated," she said, "for I shall never leave you as long as we both live."

He looked down into her face for a moment and then: "Who was An-Tak?" he asked.

"My brother," she replied. "Why?"

And then, even less than before, could he tell her. It was then that he did something he had never done before—he put his arms about her and stooping, kissed her forehead. "Until you find An-Tak," he said, "I will be your brother."

She drew away. "I already have a brother," she said, "and I do not want another."

CHAPTER FIVE

DAYS BECAME weeks, and weeks became months, and the months followed one another in a lazy procession of hot, humid days and warm, humid nights. The fugitives saw never a Wieroo by day though often at night they heard the melancholy flapping of giant wings far above them.

Each day was much like its predecessor. Bradley splashed about for a few minutes in the cold pool early each morning and after a time the girl tried it and liked it. Toward the center it was deep enough for swimming, and so he taught her to swim—she was probably the first human being in all Caspak's long ages who had done this thing. And then while she prepared breakfast, the man shaved—this he never neglected. At first it was a source of wonderment to the girl, for the Galu men are beardless.

When they needed meat, he hunted, otherwise he busied himself in improving their shelter, making new and better weapons, perfecting his knowledge of the girl's language and teaching her to speak and to write English—anything that would keep them both occupied. He still sought new plans for escape, but with ever-lessening enthusiasm, since each new scheme presented some insurmountable obstacle.

And then one day as a bolt out of a clear sky came that which blasted the peace and security of their sanctuary forever. Bradley was just emerging from the water after his morning plunge when from overhead came the sound of flapping wings. Glancing quickly up the man saw a white-robed Wieroo circling slowly above him. That he had been discovered he could not doubt since the creature even dropped to a lower altitude as though to assure itself that what it saw was a man. Then it rose rapidly and winged away toward the city.

For two days Bradley and the girl lived in a constant state of apprehension, awaiting the moment when the hunters would come for them; but nothing happened until just after dawn of the third day, when the flapping of wings apprised them of the approach of Wieroos. Together they went to the edge of the wood and looked up to see five red-robed creatures dropping slowly in ever-lessening spirals toward their little amphitheater. With no attempt at concealment they came, sure of their ability to overwhelm these two fugitives, and with the fullest measure of self-confidence they landed in the clearing but a few yards from the man and the girl.

Following a plan already discussed Bradley and the girl retreated slowly into the woods. The Wieroos advanced, calling upon them to give themselves up; but the quarry made no reply. Farther and farther into the little wood Bradley led the hunters, permitting them to approach ever closer; then he circled back again toward the clearing, evidently to the great delight of the Wieroos, who now followed more leisurely, awaiting the moment when they should be beyond the trees and able to use their wings. They had opened into semicircular formation now with the evident intention of cutting the two off from returning into the wood. Each

Wieroo advanced with his curved blade ready in his hand, each hideous face blank and expressionless.

It was then that Bradley opened fire with his pistol—three shots, aimed with careful deliberation, for it had been long since he had used the weapon, and he could not afford to chance wasting ammunition on misses. At each shot a Wieroo dropped; and then the remaining two sought escape by flight, screaming and wailing after the manner of their kind. When a Wieroo runs, his wings spread almost without any volition upon his part, since from time immemorial he has always used them to balance himself and accelerate his running speed so that in the open they appear to skim the surface of the ground when in the act of running. But here in the woods, among the close-set boles, the spreading of their wings proved their undoing—it hindered and stopped them and threw them to the ground, and then Bradley was upon them threatening them with instant death if they did not surrender—promising them their freedom if they did his bidding.

"As you have seen," he cried, "I can kill you when I wish and at a distance. You cannot escape me. Your only hope of life lies in obedience. Quick, or I kill!"

The Wieroos stopped and faced him. "What do you want of us?" asked one.

"Throw aside your weapons," Bradley commanded. After a moment's hesitation they obeyed.

"Now approach!" A great plan—the only plan—had suddenly come to him like an inspiration.

The Wieroos came closer and halted at his command. Bradley turned to the girl. "There is rope in the shelter," he said. "Fetch it!"

She did as he bid, and then he directed her to fasten one end of a fifty-foot length to the ankle of one of the Wieroos and the opposite end to the second. The creatures gave evidence of great fear, but they dared not attempt to prevent the act.

"Now go out into the clearing," said Bradley, "and remember that I am walking close behind and that I will shoot the nearer one should either attempt to escape—that will hold the other until I can kill him as well."

In the open he halted them. "The girl will get upon the back of the one in front," announced the Englishman. "I will mount the other. She carries a sharp blade, and I carry this weapon that you know kills easily at a distance. If you disobey in the slightest, the instructions that I am about to give you, you shall both die. That we must die with you, will not deter us. If you obey, I promise to set you free without harming you.

"You will carry us due west, depositing us upon the shore of the mainland—that is all. It is the price of your lives. Do you agree?"

Sullenly the Wieroos acquiesced. Bradley examined the knots that held the rope to their ankles, and feeling them secure directed the girl to mount the back of the leading Wieroo, himself upon the other. Then he gave the signal for the two to rise together. With loud flapping of the powerful wings the creatures took to the air, circling once before they topped the trees upon the hill and then taking a course due west out over the waters of the sea.

Nowhere about them could Bradley see signs of other Wieroos, nor of those other menaces which he had feared might bring disaster to his plans for escape—the huge, winged reptilia that are so numerous above the southern areas of Caspak and which are often seen, though in lesser numbers, farther north.

Nearer and nearer loomed the mainland—a broad, parklike expanse stretching inland to the foot of a low plateau spread out before them. The little dots in the foreground became grazing herds of deer and antelope and bos; a huge woolly rhinoceros wallowed in a mudhole to the right, and beyond, a mighty mammoth culled the tender shoots from a tall tree. The roars and screams and growls of giant carnivora came faintly to their ears. Ah, this was Caspak. With all of its dangers and its primal savagery it brought a fullness to the throat of the Englishmen as to one who sees and hears the familiar sights and sounds of home after a long absence. Then the Wieroos dropped swiftly downward to the flower-starred turf that grew almost to the water's edge, the fugitives slipped from their backs, and Bradley told the red-robed creatures they were free to go.

When he had cut the ropes from their ankles they rose with that uncanny wailing upon their lips that always brought a shudder to the Englishman, and upon dismal wings they flapped away toward frightful Oo-oh.

When the creatures had gone, the girl turned toward Bradley. "Why did you have them bring us here?" she asked. "Now we are far from my country. We may never live to reach it, as we are among enemies who, while not so horrible will kill us just as surely as would the Wieroos should they capture us, and we have before us many marches through lands filled with savage beasts."

"There were two reasons," replied Bradley. "You told me that there are two Wieroo cities at the eastern end of the island. To have passed near either of them might have been to have brought about our heads hundreds of the creatures from whom we could not possibly have escaped. Again, my friends must be near this spot—it cannot be over two marches to the fort of which I have told you. It is my duty to return to them. If they still live we shall find a way to return you to your people."

"And you?" asked the girl.

"I escaped from Oo-oh," replied Bradley. "I have accomplished the impossible once, and so I shall accomplish it again—I shall escape from Caspak."

He was not looking at her face as he answered her, and so he did not see the shadow of sorrow that crossed her countenance. When he raised his eyes again, she was smiling.

"What you wish, I wish," said the girl.

Southward along the coast they made their way following the beach, where the walking was best, but always keeping close enough to trees to insure sanctuary from the beasts and reptiles that so often menaced them. It was late in the afternoon when the girl suddenly seized Bradley's arm and pointed straight ahead along the shore. "What is that?" she whispered. "What strange reptile is it?"

Bradley looked in the direction her slim forefinger indicated. He rubbed his eyes and looked again, and then he seized her wrist and drew her quickly behind a clump of bushes.

"What is it?" she asked.

"It is the most frightful reptile that the waters of the world have ever known," he replied. "It is a German U-boat!"

An expression of amazement and understanding lighted her features. "It is the thing of which you told me," she exclaimed, "—the thing that swims under the water and carries men in its belly!"

"It is," replied Bradley.

"Then why do you hide from it?" asked the girl. "You said that now it belonged to your friends."

"Many months have passed since I knew what was going on among my friends," he replied. "I cannot know what has befallen them. They should have been gone from here in this vessel long since, and so I cannot understand why it is still here. I am going to investigate first before I show myself. When I left, there were more Germans on the U-33 than there were men of my own party at the fort, and I have had sufficient experience of Germans to know that they will bear watching—if they have not been properly watched since I left.

Making their way through a fringe of wood that grew a few yards inland the two crept unseen toward the U-boat which lay moored to the shore at a point which Bradley now recognized as being near the oil-pool north of Dinosaur. As close as possible to the vessel they halted, crouching low among the dense vegetation, and watched the boat for signs of human life about it. The hatches were closed—no one could be seen or heard. For five minutes Bradley watched, and then he determined to board the submarine and investigate. He had risen to carry his decision into effect when there suddenly broke upon his ear, uttered in loud and menacing tones, a volley of German oaths and expletives among which he heard *Englische schweinhunde* repeated several times. The voice did not come from the direction of the U-boat; but from inland. Creeping forward Bradley reached a spot where, through the creepers hanging from the trees, he could see a party of men coming down toward the shore.

He saw Baron Friedrich von Schoenvorts and six of his men—all armed—while marching in a little knot among them were Olson, Brady, Sinclair, Wilson, and Whitely.

Bradley knew nothing of the disappearance of Bowen Tyler and Miss La Rue, nor of the perfidy of the Germans in shelling the fort and attempting to escape in the U-33; but he was in no way surprised at what he saw before him.

The little party came slowly onward, the prisoners staggering beneath heavy cans of oil, while Schwartz, one of the German noncommissioned officers cursed and beat them with a stick of wood, impartially. Von Schoenvorts walked in the rear of the column, encouraging Schwartz and laughing at the discomfiture of the Britishers. Dietz, Heinz, and Klatz also seemed to enjoy the entertainment immensely; but two of the men—Plesser and Hindle—marched with eyes straight to the front and with scowling faces.

Bradley felt his blood boil at sight of the cowardly indignities being heaped upon his men, and in the brief span of time occupied by the column to come abreast of where he lay hidden he made his plans, foolhardy though he knew them. Then he drew the girl close to him. "Stay here," he whispered. "I am going out to fight those beasts; but I shall be killed. Do not let them see you. Do not let them take you alive. They are more cruel, more cowardly, more bestial than the Wieroos."

The girl pressed close to him, her face very white. "Go, if that is right," she whispered; "but if you die, I shall die, for I cannot live without you."

He looked sharply into her eyes. "Oh!" he ejaculated. "What an idiot I have been! Nor could I live without you, little girl." And he drew her very close and kissed her lips. "Good-bye." He disengaged himself from her arms and looked again in time to see

126

that the rear of the column had just passed him. Then he rose and leaped quickly and silently from the jungle.

Suddenly von Schoenvorts felt an arm thrown about his neck and his pistol jerked from its holster. He gave a cry of fright and warning, and his men turned to see a half-naked white man holding their leader securely from behind and aiming a pistol at them over his shoulder.

"Drop those guns!" came in short, sharp syllables and perfect German from the lips of the newcomer. "Drop them or I'll put a bullet through the back of von Schoenvorts' head."

The Germans hesitated for a moment, looking first toward von Schoenvorts and then to Schwartz, who was evidently second in command, for orders.

"It's the English pig, Bradley," shouted the latter, "and he's alone—go and get him!"

"Go yourself," growled Plesser. Hindle moved close to the side of Plesser and whispered something to him. The latter nodded. Suddenly von Schoenvorts wheeled about and seized Bradley's pistol arm with both hands, "Now!" he shouted. "Come and take him, quick!"

Schwartz and three others leaped forward; but Plesser and Hindle held back, looking questioningly toward the English prisoners. Then Plesser spoke. "Now is your chance, *Englander*," he called in low tones. "Seize Hindle and me and take our guns from us—we will not fight hard."

Olson and Brady were not long in acting upon the suggestion. They had seen enough of the brutal treatment von Schoenvorts accorded his men and the especially venomous attentions he had taken great enjoyment in according Plesser and Hindle to understand that these two might be sincere in a desire for revenge. In another moment the two Germans were unarmed and Olson and Brady were running to the support of Bradley; but already it seemed too late.

Von Schoenvorts had managed to drag the Englishman around so that his back was toward Schwartz and the other advancing Germans. Schwartz was almost upon Bradley with gun clubbed and ready to smash down upon the Englishman's skull. Brady and Olson were charging the Germans in the rear with Wilson, Whitely, and Sinclair supporting them with bare fists. It seemed that Bradley was doomed when, apparently out of space, an arrow whizzed, striking Schwartz in the side, passing half-way through his body to crumple him to earth. With a shriek the man fell, and at the same time Olson and Brady saw the slim figure of a young girl standing at the edge of the jungle coolly fitting another arrow to her bow.

Bradley had now succeeded in wrestling his arm free from von Schoenvorts' grip and in dropping the latter with a blow from the butt of his pistol. The rest of the English and Germans were engaged in a hand-to-hand encounter. Plesser and Hindle standing aside from the melee and urging their comrades to surrender and join with the English against the tyranny of von Schoenvorts. Heinz and Klatz, possibly influenced by their exhortation, were putting up but a half-hearted resistance; but Dietz, a huge, bearded, bull-necked Prussian, yelling like a maniac, sought to exterminate the *Englische schweinhunde* with his bayonet, fearing to fire his piece lest he kill some of his comrades.

It was Olson who engaged him, and though unused to the long German rifle and bayonet, he met the bull-rush of the Hun with the cold, cruel precision and science of English bayonet-fighting. There was no feinting, no retiring and no parrying that was not also an attack. Bayonet-fighting today is not a pretty thing to see—it is no artistic fencing-match in which men give and take—it is slaughter inevitable and quickly over.

Dietz lunged once madly at Olson's throat. A short point, with just a twist of the bayonet to the left sent the sharp blade over the Englishman's left shoulder. Instantly he stepped close in, dropped his rifle through his hands and grasped it with both close below the muzzle and with a short, sharp jab sent his blade up beneath Dietz's chin clear to the brain. So quickly was the thing done and so quick the withdrawal that Olson had wheeled to take on another adversary before the German's corpse had toppled to the ground.

But there were no more adversaries to take on. Heinz and Klatz had thrown down their rifles and with hands above their heads were crying "Kamerad! Kamerad!" at the tops of their voices. Von Schoenvorts still lay where he had fallen. Plesser and Hindle were explaining to Bradley that they were glad of the outcome of the fight, as they could no longer endure the brutality of the U-boat commander.

The remainder of the men were looking at the girl who now advanced slowly, her bow ready, when Bradley turned toward her and held out his hand.

"Co-Tan," he said, "unstring your bow—these are my friends, and yours." And to the Englishmen: "This is Co-Tan. You who saw her save me from Schwartz know a part of what I owe her."

The rough men gathered about the girl, and when she spoke to them in broken English, with a smile upon her lips enhancing the charm of her irresistible accent, each and every one of them promptly fell in love with her and constituted himself henceforth her guardian and her slave.

A moment later the attention of each was called to Plesser by a volley of invective. They turned in time to see the man running toward von Schoenvorts who was just rising from the ground. Plesser carried a rifle with bayonet fixed, that he had snatched from the side of Dietz's corpse. Von Schoenvorts' face was livid with fear, his jaws working as though he would call for help; but no sound came from his blue lips.

"You struck me," shrieked Plesser. "Once, twice, three times, you struck me, pig. You murdered Schwerke—you drove him insane by your cruelty until he took his own life. You are only one of your kind —they are all like you from the Kaiser down. I wish that you were the Kaiser. Thus would I do!" And he lunged his bayonet through von Schoenvorts' chest. Then he let his rifle fall with the dying man and wheeled toward Bradley. "Here I am," he said. "Do with me as you like. All my life I have been kicked and cuffed by such as that, and yet always have I gone out when they commanded, singing, to give up my life if need be to keep them in power. Only lately have I come to know what a fool I have been. But now I am no longer a fool, and besides, I am avenged and Schwerke is avenged, so you can kill me if you wish. Here I am."

"If I was after bein' the king," said Olson, "I'd pin the V.C. on your noble chist; but bein' only an Irishman with a Swede name, for which God forgive me, the bist I can do is shake your hand."

"You will not be punished," said Bradley. "There are four of you left—if you four want to come along and work with us, we will take you; but you will come as prisoners."

"It suits me," said Plesser. "Now that the captain-lieutenant is dead you need not fear us. All our lives we have known nothing but to obey his class. If I had not killed him, I suppose I would be fool enough to obey him again; but he is dead. Now we will obey you—we must obey some one."

"And you?" Bradley turned to the other survivors of the original crew of the U-33. Each promised obedience.

The two dead Germans were buried in a single grave, and then the party boarded the submarine and stowed away the oil.

Here Bradley told the men what had befallen him since the night of September 14th when he had disappeared so mysteriously from the camp upon the plateau. Now he learned for the first time that Bowen J. Tyler, Jr., and Miss La Rue had been missing even longer than he and that no faintest trace of them had been discovered.

Olson told him of how the Germans had returned and waited in ambush for them outside the fort, capturing them that they might be used to assist in the work of refining the oil and later in manning the U-33, and Plesser told briefly of the experiences of the German crew under von Schoenvorts since they had escaped from Caspak months before—of how they lost their bearings after having been shelled by ships they had attempted to sneak farther north and how at last with provisions gone and fuel almost exhausted they had sought and at last found, more by accident than design, the mysterious island they had once been so glad to leave behind.

"Now," announced Bradley, "we'll plan for the future. The boat has fuel, provisions and water for a month, I believe you said, Plesser; there are ten of us to man it. We have a last sad duty here—we must search for Miss La Rue and Mr. Tyler. I say a sad duty because we know that we shall not find them; but it is none the less our duty to comb the shore-line, firing signal shells at internals, that we at least may leave at last with full knowledge that we have done all that men might do to locate them."

None dissented from this conviction, nor was there a voice raised in protest against the plan to at least make assurance doubly sure before quitting Caspak forever.

And so they started, cruising slowly up the coast and firing an occasional shot from the gun. Often the vessel was brought to a stop, and always there were anxious eyes scanning the shore for an answering signal. Late in the afternoon they caught sight of a number of Band-lu warriors; but when the vessel approached the shore and the natives realized that human beings stood upon the back of the strange monster of the sea, they fled in terror before Bradley could come within hailing distance.

That night they dropped anchor at the mouth of a sluggish stream whose warm waters swarmed with millions of tiny tadpolelike organisms—minute human spawn starting on their precarious journey from some inland pool toward "the beginning"—a journey which one in millions, perhaps, might survive to complete. Already almost at the inception of life they were being greeted by thousands of voracious mouths as fish and reptiles of many kinds fought to devour them, the while other and larger creatures pursued the devourers, to be, in turn, preyed upon by some other of the countless forms that inhabit the deeps of Caprona's frightful sea.

The second day was practically a repetition of the first. They moved very slowly with frequent stops and once they landed in the Kro-lu country to hunt. Here they were attacked by the bow-and-arrow men, whom they could not persuade to palaver with them. So belligerent were the natives that it became necessary to fire into them in order to escape their persistent and ferocious attentions.

"What chance," asked Bradley, as they were returning to the boat with their game, "could Tyler and Miss La Rue have had among such as these?"

But they continued on their fruitless quest, and the third day, after cruising along the shore of a deep inlet, they passed a line of lofty cliffs that formed the southern shore of the inlet and rounded a sharp promontory about noon. Co-Tan and Bradley were on deck alone, and as the new shoreline appeared beyond the point, the girl gave an exclamation of joy and seized the man's hand in hers.

"Oh, look!" she cried. "The Galu country! The Galu country! It is my country that I never thought to see again."

"You are glad to come again. Co-Tan?" asked Bradley.

"Oh, so glad!" she cried. "And you will come with me to my people? We may live here among them, and you will be a great warrior—oh, when Jor dies you may even be chief, for there is none so mighty as my warrior. You will come?"

Bradley shook his head. "I cannot, little Co-Tan," he answered. "My country needs me, and I must go back. Maybe someday I shall return. You will not forget me, Co-Tan?"

She looked at him in wide-eyed wonder. "You are going away from me?" she asked in a very small voice. "You are going away from Co-Tan?"

Bradley looked down upon the little bowed head. He felt the soft cheek against his bare arm; and he felt something else there too—hot drops of moisture that ran down to his very finger-tips and splashes, but each one wrung from a woman's heart.

He bent low and raised the tear-stained face to his own. "No, Co-Tan," he said, "I am not going away from you—for you are going with me. You are going back to my own country to be my wife. Tell me that you will, Co-Tan." And he bent still lower yet from his height and kissed her lips. Nor did he need more than the wonderful new light in her eyes to tell him that she would go to the end of the world with him if he would but take her. And then the gun-crew came up from below again to fire a signal shot, and the two were brought down from the high heaven of their new happiness to the scarred and weather-beaten deck of the U-33.

An hour later the vessel was running close in by a shore of wondrous beauty beside a parklike meadow that stretched back a mile inland to the foot of a plateau when Whitely called attention to a score of figures clambering downward from the elevation to the lowland below. The engines were reversed and the boat brought to a stop while all hands gathered on deck to watch the little party coming toward them across the meadow.

"They are Galus," cried Co-Tan; "they are my own people. Let me speak to them lest they think we come to fight them. Put me ashore, my man, and I will go meet them."

The nose of the U-boat was run close in to the steep bank; but when Co-Tan would have run forward alone, Bradley seized her hand and held her back. "I will go with you, Co-Tan," he said; and together they advanced to meet the oncoming party.

There were about twenty warriors moving forward in a thin line, as our infantry advance as skirmishers. Bradley could not but notice the marked difference between this formation and the moblike methods of the lower tribes he had come in contact with, and he commented upon it to Co-Tan."

"Galu warriors always advance into battle thus," she said. "The lesser people remain in a huddled group where they can scarce use their weapons the while they present so big a mark to us that our spears and arrows cannot miss them; but when they hurl theirs at our warriors, if they miss the first man, there is no chance that they will kill some one behind him.

"Stand still now," she cautioned, "and fold your arms. They will not harm us then."

Bradley did as he was bid, and the two stood with arms folded as the line of warriors approached. When they had come within some fifty yards, they halted and one spoke. "Who are you and from whence do you come?" he asked; and then Co-Tan gave a little, glad cry and sprang forward with outstretched arms.

"Oh, Tan!" she exclaimed. "Do you know know your little Co-Tan?"

The warrior stared, incredulous, for a moment, and then he, too, ran forward and when they met, took the girl in his arms. It was then that Bradley experienced to the full a sensation that was new to him—a sudden hatred for the strange warrior before him and a desire to kill without knowing why he would kill. He moved quickly to the girl's side and grasped her wrist.

"Who is this man?" he demanded in cold tones.

Co-Tan turned a surprised face toward the Englishman and then of a sudden broke forth into a merry peal of laughter. "This is my father, Bradlee," she cried.

"And who is Brad-lee?" demanded the warrior.

"He is my man," replied Co-Tan simply.

"By what right?" insisted Tan.

And then she told him briefly of all that she had passed through since the Wieroos had stolen her and of how Bradley had rescued her and sought to rescue An-Tak, her brother.

"You are satisfied with him?" asked Tan.

"Yes," replied the girl proudly.

It was then that Bradley's attention was attracted to the edge of the plateau by a movement there, and looking closely he saw a horse bearing two figures sliding down the steep declivity. Once at the bottom, the animal came charging across the meadowland at a rapid run. It was a magnificent animal—a great bay stallion with a white-blazed face and white forelegs to the knees, its barrel encircled by a broad surcingle of white; and as it came to a sudden stop beside Tan, the Englishman saw that it bore a man and a girl—a tall man and a girl as beautiful as Co-Tan. When the girl espied the latter, she slid from the horse and ran toward her, fairly screaming for joy.

The man dismounted and stood beside Tan. Like Bradley he was garbed after the fashion of the surrounding warriors; but there was a subtle difference between him and his companion. Possibly he detected a similar difference in Bradley, for his first question was; "From what country?" and though he spoke in Galu Bradley thought he detected an accent.

"England," replied Bradley.

A broad smile lighted the newcomer's face as he

held out his hand. "I am Tom Billings of Santa Monica, California," he said. "I know all about you, and I'm mighty glad to find you alive."

"How did you get here?" asked Bradley. "I thought ours was the only party of men from the outer world ever to enter Caprona."

"It was, until we came in search of Bowen J. Tyler, Jr.," replied Billings. "We found him and sent him home with his bride; but I was kept a prisoner here."

Bradley's face darkened—then they were not among friends after all. "There are ten of us down there on a German sub with small-arms and a gun," he said quickly in English. "It will be no trick to get away from these people."

"You don't know my jailer," replied Billings, "or you'd not be so sure. Wait, I'll introduce you." And then turning to the girl who had accompanied him he called her by name. "Ajor," he said, "permit me to introduce Lieutenant Bradley; Lieutenant, Mrs. Billings—my jailer!"

The Englishman laughed as he shook hands with the girl. "You are not as good a soldier as I," he said to Billings. "Instead of being taken prisoner myself I have taken one—Mrs. Bradley, this is Mr. Billings."

Ajor, quick to understand, turned toward Co-Tan. "You are going back with him to his country?" she asked. Co-Tan admitted it.

"You dare?" asked Ajor. "But your father will not permit it—Jor, my father, High Chief of the Galus, will not permit it, for like me you are *cos-ata-lo*. Oh, Co-Tan, if we but could! How I would love to see all the strange and wonderful things of which my Tom tells me!"

Bradley bent and whispered in her ear. "Say the word and you may both go with us."

Billings heard and speaking in English, asked Ajor if she would go.

"Yes," she answered, "if you wish it; but you know, my Tom, that if Jor captures us, both you and Co-Tan's man will pay the penalty with your lives—not even his love for me nor his admiration for you can save you."

Bradley noticed that she spoke in English—broken English like Co-Tan's but equally appealing. "We can easily get you aboard the ship," he said, "on some pretext or other, and then we can steam away. They can neither harm nor detain us, nor will we have to fire a shot at them."

And so it was done, Bradley and Co-Tan taking Ajor and Billings aboard to "show" them the vessel, which almost immediately raised anchor and moved slowly out into the sea.

"I hate to do it," said Billings. "They have been fine to me. Jor and Tan are splendid men and they will think me an ingrate; but I can't waste my life here when there is so much to be done in the outer world."

As they steamed down the inland sea past the island of Oo-oh, the stories of their adventures were retold, and Bradley learned that Bowen Tyler and his bride had left the Galu country but a fortnight before and that there was every reason to believe that the *Toreador* might still be lying in the Pacific not far off the subterranean mouth of the river which emitted Caprona's heated waters into the ocean.

Late in the second day, after running through swarms of hideous reptiles, they submerged at the point where the river entered beneath the cliffs and shortly after rose to the sunlit surface of the Pacific; but nowhere as far as they could see was sign of another craft. Down the coast they steamed toward the beach where Billings had made his crossing in the hydro-aeroplane and just at dusk the lookout announced a light dead ahead. It proved to be aboard the *Toreador*, and a half-hour later there was such a reunion on the deck of the trig little yacht as no one there had ever dreamed might be possible. Of the Allies there were only Tippet and James to be mourned, and no one mourned any of the German dead nor Benson, the traitor, whose ugly story was first told in Bowen Tyler's manuscript.

Tyler and the rescue party had but just reached the yacht that afternoon. They had heard, faintly, the signal shots fired by the U-33 but had been unable to locate their direction and so had assumed that they had come from the guns of the *Toreador*.

It was a happy party that sailed north toward sunny, southern California, the old U-33 trailing in the wake of the *Toreador* and flying with the latter the glorious Stars and Stripes beneath which she had been born in the shipyard at Santa Monica. Three newly married couples, their bonds now duly solemnized by the master of the ship, joyed in the peace and security of the untracked waters of the south Pacific and the unique honeymoon which, had it not been for stern duty ahead, they could have wished protracted till the end of time.

And so they came one day to dock at the shipyard which Bowen Tyler now controlled, and here the U-33 still lies while those who passed so many eventful days within and because of her, have gone their various ways.

Edgar Rice Burroughs is one of the world's most popular authors. Although not fully recognised by some critics and libraries, he remains one of the best known American fiction writers of the 20th century. With no previous experience as an author, he wrote the renown classic TARZAN OF THE APES, first published in 1912. In the ensuing forty-two years, he wrote over 100 stories and articles, nearly all of which were published during his lifetime. Although best known for creating TARZAN, his worlds of adventure and romance ranged from the American West to the jungles of Asia, from inside the earth on to the moon, Mars, Venus and even beyond the farthest star.

No one knows how many copies of ERB's 68 books have been published throughout the world. It is conservative to say, however, that of the translations into 31 languages in addition to the artificial languages of Esperanto and Braille, the total number must run into the hundreds of millions. When one considers the additional world-wide following of the Tarzan newspaper feature, radio programs, comic magazines, motion pictures and television series, Burroughs must be known by a thousand million people.

Whether you are about to read an adventure on Mars, a romance of the jungle, or a fantasy of the future, the magic of the prolific imagination of Edgar Rice Burroughs will hold you spellbound for a long time to come.

✿　✿　✿

Attesting to the unparalleled following of Edgar Rice Burroughs, a club and several magazines are managed by dedicated ERB admirers, who publish information, discussions and art on Burroughs and his creations. Interested readers are invited to inquire for further information from:

The Burroughs Bibliophiles (club), 6657 Locust St., Kansas City, Mo. 64131

ERB-dom (magazine), P.O. Box 550, Evergreen, Colo. 80439

The Barsoomian (magazine), 84 Charlton Road, Rochester, N.Y. 14617

ERBANIA (magazine), 8001 Fernview Lane, Tampa, Fla. 33615

ANDRE NORTON

696823	Quest Crosstime	75c
749812	Sargasso of Space	75c
756957	Sea Siege	75c
758318	Secret of the Lost Race	75c
759910	Shadow Hawk	75c
768010	The Sioux Spaceman	60c
775510	Sorceress of Witch World	75c
780114	Star Born	75c
780718	Star Gate	60c
781914	Star Hunter & Voodoo Planet	60c
784314	The Stars Are Ours	75c
787416	Storm over Warlock	60c
808014	Three Against the Witch World	75c
812511	The Time Traders	60c
863217	Victory On Janus	75c
873190	Warlock of the Witch World	60c
878710	Web of the Witch World	75c
897017	Witch World	60c
925511	The X Factor	75c
942516	Year of the Unicorn	60c
959619	The Zero Stone	75c

Available wherever paperbacks are sold or use this coupon.

EDGAR RICE
BURROUGHS

Just 75c Each

092023	Carson of Venus
092825	Cave Girl
215624	Escape on Venus
470211	Land Time Forgot
492926	The Lost Continent
495028	Lost on Venus
537027	Moon Maid
537522	Moon Men
644823	Out of Time's Abyss
665026	The Pirates of Venus
798520	Tarzan at the Earth's Core

Available wherever paperbacks are sold or use this coupon.